A CANDLELIGHT ROMANCE

CANDLELIGHT ROMANCES

OMEN
FOR LOVE

Esther Boyd

A CANDLELIGHT ROMANCE

Published by
Dell Publishing Co., Inc.
1 Dag Hammarskjold Plaza
New York, New York 10017

Dell ® TM 681510, Dell Publishing Co., Inc.

ISBN: 0-440-16108-8

Printed in the United States of America

First printing—March 1980

Chapter 1

Carol Baxter stood in the empty opera house, pleased to have discovered its vast, cool space. After being in the sunlight, she was at first only dimly aware of the rows of red plush seats, the gilded boxes, and the heavy curtains, drawn back to reveal a bare wooden stage.

The silence enveloped her like a cocoon. In the refreshing semidarkness she had at last found a refuge from the oppressive heat outside. A place to think. A place to recover from a hurt. An unlikely place, for sure, a disused opera house in the middle of a jungle city. But Manaus was like that. Tropical inertia and decay had all but eroded the marvels of its heyday nearly a century ago.

Now there was little left. The great theater was one of the few remaining relics of the days when Manaus was rich and gay. Days when rubber was king and men made fortunes from the jungle trees, spending their gold on lavish entertainment and riding the hot, dusty streets in custom-made carriages. At that time the whole world's supply of rubber had come from the plantations that surrounded the city.

For Carol the opera house made a perfect place to think over the bewildering succession of events that had overturned her life in the two short weeks since Christmas Day. It was those events that had brought her to Manaus, isolated except by air from every other corner of civilization, a thousand miles up the Amazon River.

The atmosphere in the deserted auditorium soothed her ragged nerves. She could easily imagine the lords and ladies of that bygone era, dressed in their frock coats and billowing dresses, raptly watching the latest production, imported at unbelievable expense in some great sailing ship. The Europeans who lived in this Brazilian town, she mused, may well have come here to escape from something or someone in their homelands. If so, she felt a kindred spirit with them, as she too was here to escape. She was fleeing from a way of life that she had almost allowed herself to be drawn into back home in Albany, New York State—a life that she had recognized as destined for calamity only just in time. A life with Edward.

The crisis had come on Christmas morning. Slumping into an aisle seat, Carol relived that awful, impetuous moment when she had stormed out of his apartment. The seat clanged as it folded down under her weight, and the sound echoed through the lofty chambers above her. She tossed back her mane of auburn hair and peered into the recesses. She saw the scene as vividly as if it were being performed on the stage.

Edward had thanked her for her present to him and had now produced his gift to her, a painting by one of Albany's controversial artists, a friend of his. Edward admired both the man and his work, but he knew full well that Carol didn't care for either. As she had stared at it, nervously fingering the wrapping paper, not knowing what to say, he had told her the reason he had bought it for her.

"To teach you, my love, to appreciate what is good art. When we get married, we will hang it in a prominent place in the living room. In time you will come to recognize its quality."

"But . . . but, Edward," she had said, "I don't like it. You knew before you bought it that I didn't like it. Can't you see that I never will? I couldn't bear to live with it every day. . . ."

"You'll change your mind after a while," he had said with almost a sneer of condescension. And that was the moment when Carol had realized that the gift bore the stamp of Edward's character as surely as if he had given her an expensive men's suit for him to wear himself. She had been on the verge of condemning herself to live with this arrogant, selfish, overbearing boor for the rest of her life; she ran screaming from his apartment and spent the rest of Christmas Day locked in her own small flat, worrying about what she had done.

Her family, her friends, even Edward himself, had beseeched her to change her mind. But Carol had been adamant. She had turned her back forever on her handsome, successful fiancé, refusing to become the sort of woman whose life is dominated by her husband's tastes.

Only days later she had started looking for a job as far away from Albany as possible. She was a nurse, a nurse with special training in public health, and she soon found an opening near a town in Peru called Iquitos. The position had been advertised by a Dr. Ian Morrison, also from New York. Dr. Morrison was working temporarily for a charitable organization in a camp among the Indians of the Amazon region; an outbreak of measles had occurred, and he needed a public health nurse immediately to carry out an immunization program on the natives.

Carol had applied and been accepted. Yesterday she had flown directly from New York to Manaus; now she was patiently waiting until the day after tomorrow when a plane would take her farther up the Amazon, over the border from Brazil into Peru, and put her down in Iquitos.

Meanwhile, here she sat in the opera house, collecting her thoughts and beginning to regain her peace with the world. . . .

Carol nearly jumped out of her seat when the stage in front of her suddenly leaped into dazzling light. A moment later a tall, slim man strode purposefully out from the wings and took up his stance behind the footlights. After an elaborate low bow to Carol, he flung his arms above his head and burst into song.

His face looked pale without make-up, but she could see that he was good-looking with a long straight nose and flecks of gray in his curly black hair. His strong voice rang through the theater as he gesticulated with the passion of his rhapsody. It wasn't a bad tenor voice, Carol had to admit, but she felt outraged at having her precious peace

7

shattered by his intrusion. The song he was singing added to her annoyance.

"*La donna è mobil-ay! La donna è mobil-ay!*" Each powerful syllable seemed to be directed straight at her.

She recognized the popular aria from Verdi's opera *Rigoletto*. She also knew the English translation. "All women are fickle! All women are fickle!" The words did nothing to help her get over the sense of guilt that had plagued her since she had walked out on Edward.

The man stopped singing and bowed to her again. Then, when she made no move, he loudly applauded himself. Perhaps he doesn't know I'm here, she thought. If I just keep still he'll finish his little game of make-believe and go away, leaving me in peace once more. He was obviously a tourist, dressed as he was in a white T-shirt, jeans, and sandals, but what nationality she couldn't guess, not South American anyway.

"Didn't you like that?" he called from the stage. "Perhaps this one will suit you better."

His hands flew into the air, and he plunged into another aria, which was unfamiliar to Carol. She had a very minimal interest in opera. "*Mimi è una civetta,*" he sang. "*Che frascheggia con tutti!*" He stopped, shading his eyes from the glare, and called out to her again. "Don't you know that one either? It's from Puccini's *La Bohème* and means, 'Mimi's just a flirt, toying with all the men.' I thought that might appeal to you."

This was the last straw. Angrily she rose from her seat and stalked toward the entrance. But she heard him leap over the footlights and come running up the aisle after her. He caught up with her in the lobby just inside the main door.

"Oh, don't run out on my concert," he said, gripping her arm and grinning broadly, "I do much better with an audience."

"Let go of me!" Carol spat at him, although she couldn't help noticing that he was even more handsome than she had thought when he smiled, and he certainly had a beautiful physique of powerful muscles under his T-shirt.

"What's the matter? Don't you like opera? Even in this fabulous old place? Can't you imagine what it was like when it was new and the famous stars from Europe sang here?" The fascination in his tone softened Carol a little, but she was still furious.

"You have no right to come in here and disturb the peace, especially with those . . . those songs about women. And if you want to know, no, I don't particularly like opera."

"Not like opera?" He clapped a hand dramatically to his forehead. "You should like it! It's great! Once you've gotten to know a few . . ."

Shades of Edward. "Don't you dare tell me what I should like and what I shouldn't like," she said through clenched teeth. "I'm perfectly capable of making up my own mind, thank you."

"But that's absurd!" he argued. "If you've never tried . . ."

"How do you know I've never tried it? I happened to recognize the aria from *Rigoletto* you sang first . . . in spite of your terrible voice."

He laughed outright now, showing very white teeth against the tan of his face. "Okay, so I'm not another Caruso. But I could teach you to like opera. What's your name?"

"It's none of your business," she replied haughtily, "and it so happens I don't even *want* to like your music. I'm sick of people trying to teach me to like what they like. And now, if it gives you any satisfaction, you've completely ruined what could have been quite a nice afternoon. Good-bye."

She turned to go, but he grabbed her arm again. "I'm sorry," he said. "Let's go and have some coffee and talk about something else. There can't be more than half a dozen tourists in this whole town . . ."

Carol shook herself free. "I'd rather be by myself, thank you. If your inflated ego can conceive of such a thing."

"Hey, wait a minute . . ." he called, but she was already out of the door into the scorching heat again, her auburn hair glinting in the sunlight as it bobbed on her

9

shoulders with every step down the long flight to the street.

She hurried along, her heels clicking determinedly on the flagstones until she came to the next corner. Then, while crossing the road, she sneaked a glance back to the opera house. Thank goodness he wasn't following her. He was standing at the top of the steps, his hands in his pockets, laughing his head off . . .

Her rage at the arrogant stranger still bubbling within her, she wandered along the edge of the canal running through the city, her mind only vaguely on where she was going. Surely all good-looking men weren't so insufferable, she thought. So why did she have to run into them wherever she went? The man whom she had just met seemed to have all of Edward's charm and looks, but also, unfortunately, his total lack of consideration for other people's feelings. But, she had to admit, he had shown more sense of humor than Edward ever had, and he hadn't even been annoyed when she was rude about his voice. Perhaps he wasn't as bad as he seemed. Anyway, she'd never see him again, so what did it matter?

She could feel her blouse getting damp with the humidity of the afternoon and turned her steps toward her hotel. Manaus was a lazy place at this time of day. A few swarthy-looking men lounged in doorways, eyeing her as she passed, an occasional group of children played desultorily on the sidewalk, and some dogs padded along on business of their own; but otherwise all was quiet. She collected her key from the sleepy porter in her hotel foyer and went up to her room to think some more and wonder how she was going to kill tomorrow.

Next morning the clerk at the hotel desk decided for Carol how she was to spend her last day in Manaus. There was really only one thing to do if you had already walked around the town and seen the opera house. That was to take the guided bus tour into the neighboring countryside. Only two roads led out of the city, one toward the old rubber plantations, the other along the north bank of the Amazon, each about twenty miles long. The bus went out along the first and then cut through on a track to meet the other, coming back along it to the city again. It was very interesting, the clerk assured her in his broken English.

At ten o'clock she climbed aboard the minibus outside her hotel. She had put on a crisp pair of white pants, which fitted neatly over her slim hips, and a blue striped stretchy tube top, which left her shoulders and arms bare. To add a little dash she tied a small blue silk scarf around her throat. After a New York winter she felt her skin to be strangely pale beside the dark color of the Portuguese-Indian population of Manaus. A few weeks of this sunshine, though, and she'd soon have a nice tan.

The only other occupants of the bus when it drew away from the hotel were an elderly German couple who talked to each other in a series of muffled grunts. However, the driver, who spoke better English than the hotel clerk, told her that they had another passenger to pick up at a different hotel. Carol hoped it would be someone more companionable than the Germans. Otherwise she might have to spend the next four hours fending off the driver, who had already looked her over appreciatively and appeared all set to engage her in a steady stream of conversation. She never could stand nosy strangers who wanted to know everything about her at first sight.

The bus stopped outside a smaller hotel, and Carol didn't know whether to be relieved or distressed when she saw that the other passenger was to be the opera-loving gentleman of yesterday afternoon.

He climbed aboard, nodding casually to Carol as though it was the most natural thing in the world for her to be on the bus too. After exchanging a word with the driver, he looked at Carol quizzically, wondering whether to sit with her or not. She shrugged and allowed him a faint smile that decided the issue. He came over and dropped onto the seat beside her. Carol noticed with relief that he left a full foot of space between them.

"Thanks for the encouragement," he said. "I was afraid you were going to scare me into sitting way at the back by myself."

"I will if you as much as mention opera," she replied.

"Scout's honor," he promised. "For the duration of this trip, it never existed as an art form. Satisfied?"

11

His gray eyes met her hazel ones and crinkled humorously at the corners. Perhaps he wasn't so bad after all, she thought. At least she'd give him the benefit of the doubt.

"You look sharp in that outfit," he said glancing admiringly at the strip of skin between her top and her pants. "Manaus isn't much used to American fashions, you know. Just as well I got on—the driver would have been propositioning you from here back to here again." The driver had in fact adopted a rather surly expression since they had started talking.

"I hope I'm safer with you," she said.

"Absolutely. I have my own honey, to whom I am ever faithful. Now tell me, what part of the States do you hail from?—no, let me guess . . . I'd say California, San Francisco."

"You could hardly be more wrong. I'm from Albany. In New York State, in case you've never heard of it."

"Well, isn't that a coincidence! I was brought up in New York, but I've been in Houston the last few years. That's in far-off Texas, in case you've never heard of it."

Oh, here goes the smart aleck again, thought Carol. I'm not giving away another thing about myself. She turned to stare out of the window. The houses were thinning out now, and the forest was beginning to take over. Thick, luscious undergrowth had already begun to reclaim areas that had once been cultivated or built on and later been abandoned. Nature was encroaching again.

"And what would a young lady from dear old Albany, New York, be doing in Manaus?" He was asking questions again.

"I'm in Manaus getting my first taste of jungle life. Tomorrow I fly away. To somewhere else. And that's all the answer you're going to get."

"Oh, tell me where you're going. I'm interested . . . honestly I am. You see, you might just be . . ."

"No," Carol said firmly. "Now tell *me* what all those trees are, the great tall ones with thick trunks and masses of leaves up at the top."

"Nuts!" he said. "No, I don't mean you—I mean that's

12

what those trees are. Brazil nuts. Here, if you've never seen them growing, I'll show you." He tapped the driver on the shoulder and the bus stopped. They jumped out and walked over to the nearest tall tree. Far up in the branches Carol could see some brownish green pods the size of coconuts. On the ground below were one or two that had fallen down. Kneeling, she opened a husk where it had already begun to split. Inside were four neat rows of eight wedge-shaped black Brazil nuts, all fitting together to make a circle. Exactly thirty-two nuts to each husk.

"This is fascinating," she said, pulling the nuts off one by one. "Look at how they're . . ." But she was talking to thin air. Her guide had vanished. Momentarily panicked, she saw the bus was still parked and the Germans were stretching their legs. Then she spotted the other passenger, nimbly leaping down from a branch. He advanced toward her and handed her a delicate pink and white flower. She stood up to take it from him.

"Has anyone ever given you an orchid before?" he asked. "If not, may I have the pleasure. One genuine wild orchid, though not a very rare species, I'm afraid."

"Thank you," Carol said graciously. "No, this really is a first for me. It's beautiful." She examined its delicacy.

"But you've seen them before, I'm sure. Possibly by some patient's bedside in the hospital where you work as a nurse. Or maybe you don't work in a hospital anymore. Would you be in public health by any chance?" He asked the question with a curious new inflection in his voice.

Carol lowered the flower from her face and stared at him. "How did you know I was a nurse? Nobody ever takes me for one when I'm out of uniform. Especially not as a public health nurse."

"So I was right, was I? You are one." He let out an unexpected sigh, and his expression suddenly changed from that of a jocular fellow tourist enjoying a mild flirtation to one of polite reserve.

"Yes, but what's the matter with that?" she asked. "Don't you like nurses or something?"

"It's all right, you needn't be offended. I like nurses very much as a matter of fact. They can be extremely useful people. I know, because I've been around them quite a bit."

"Why? Have you recently been sick? You look fit enough now. Who are you and what are you doing in Manaus?"

He shook his head, looking serious to the point of sadness. "No questions, remember. I never discuss personal matters with strangers."

"Touché," she shrugged. "But it's weird you knowing what my profession is. Okay, let's get back to the bus."

Farther on they stopped to look at a waterfall. It plunged down in a foaming torrent between luxuriant green ferns into a calm pool of clear water dotted with giant water lilies. It looked like a set piece from some cleverly designed botanical gardens. Carol loved it; she always wanted to bathe in a waterfall whenever she saw one. In her pleasure at the sight, she touched her companion's arm, but he shied away as if he had been stung. Embarrassed, she drew back.

The driver was explaining that a large flat stone in the middle of the pool was a favorite spot for voodoo ceremonies. Candles flickered here, he told them, on nights of the full moon, women went into trances, and men gained the power of second sight.

"That's my secret," said the man beside her, "voodoo. At the last full moon I was told I was doomed to meet a nurse on a tour bus."

"What did your 'honey' have to say to that?" teased Carol, egged on by his joke. "And how come she isn't here with you on your sightseeing?"

"Oh, I'm just in Manaus on business. A firm in Rio is sending me some valuable cargo on tomorrow's flight. Then I must leave. I have work to do—and so presumably have you. So you get on with yours and I'll get on with mine. That way it'll be better for both of us."

Carol turned away. Why had this man suddenly become so cold and distant, all involved in work? She had thought he was fun before—even the crazy scene in the opera house had taken her mind off Edward, and that was what she was here for. Today he didn't remind her of Edward at all. He was much nicer—or had been until this odd change of mood—and better looking too. Too bad she wasn't going to see him again. Tomorrow he'd be on his way to Houston with his precious cargo, whatever it was.

The bus stopped once more, beside a pebbly beach on the bank of the Amazon. This was Carol's first ground-level view of the immense river whose far shore was no more than a faint haze of green more than a mile away. She felt insignificantly small before its immutable grandeur; it made her want to seek human contact. But the German couple was arguing in the back seat of the bus, and the driver had gone into a nearby café to chat with some friends.

Her only other fellow-traveler was squatting on his haunches, idly throwing stones into the water. He looked up as she approached, a long look that made her feel uncomfortable, and then returned to hurling rocks into the river with new concentration.

"The size of this river knocks you over," she said brightly.

"You'll get used to it," he replied in a flat disinterested tone.

"You must know it well," she tried again, thinking that she had caught him in a morose frame of mind, and she should try to cheer him up.

"Well enough. And so will you after you've worked near it for a while. Don't let it turn your head, that's all. It's only a river."

"I didn't say I was going to work by the Amazon," she said.

"Didn't you?" he answered with a wan smile, as he again looked her up and down in that disconcerting way. "I told you I'm psychic."

On the last leg of the tour, down the river and into the city, he sat beside her but remained silent. What has happened to his cheerful personality? she wondered. I hope it isn't anything to do with me.

"Nearly home for you now," he remarked, breaking the long void. "Your hotel's around the next corner. The bus'll take me on to mine."

15

"Well, thanks for your company—and the orchid. And your opera singing wasn't really that bad," she smiled. He looked so sad.

"Next time I'll try and do better"—absurd remark, thought Carol, as if there could ever be a next time—"I'll learn some new arias for you, ones that don't offend women's lib."

She touched his shoulder as she got out of the bus. This time he didn't cringe, but grinned at her out of the window, more himself again. "Bye, Carol Baxter," he called after her as the vehicle drew away.

Dumfounded, Carol stood by the curb, the orchid held limply in her hand, until the bus had passed out of sight. How on earth could he have known her name? She realized with annoyance that she had had to think of him as a nameless stranger all afternoon, while he had known all along what she was called and what her job was. He might even have known about Iquitos. She felt at a hopeless disadvantage.

She went slowly into the hotel and up to the desk. "Excuse me, but . . . did anybody phone here this morning—or last night—to ask my name?" she inquired of the clerk.

The clerk shook his head uncomprehendingly. "Phone for you, miss? No, no phone for you. No phone at all."

Reasoning made her check her purse for any means of identification, in case he had taken a look into it on the bus. Up in her room she checked there too, but her passport and her plane ticket were in the hotel safe, and there was nothing else lying around with her name on it. It was uncanny, inexplicable.

Although the hotel dining room wasn't very elegant, she put on her best short dress for dinner that night, a cool, sleeveless, linen one. There was just a chance that he might reappear. He? Why did she have to think of him just as "he"? Darn it, why did she have to think of him at all! She told herself that she was being a silly girl on a rebound, an easy target for the first halfway good-looking man to come along. She determined to put him and his stupid tricks out of her mind.

Vigorously she attacked the whole grilled fish that the waiter put before her, and haughtily ignored the stares of a mustachioed Brazilian who was eating by himself at the next table. She left the room without waiting for dessert and went upstairs to pack. Her plane left early in the morning—the plane that was going to take her into the real jungle world, that was going to be her home for the next few months. The place where she was going to work hard at saving lives and savoring a whole new environment, far from the Albany Health Unit, far from her reproachful parents and friends, and above all far from Edward. She vowed that she wasn't going to think of any man except in a platonic way until the shattering experience of Christmas had become a distant memory.

The plane from Manaus to Iquitos was propeller driven and scheduled to take three hours, but it was late starting. Eventually it took off, and Carol's seat by the window afforded her a spectacular view during the flight. The enormous brown river below meandered back and forth through the unbroken expanse of dark green jungle, looking like deep-pile broadloom from the air. Sometimes it strayed so far from the straight line of the plane's flight path that it disappeared far into the distant haze, only to wind its way back underneath a few minutes later. Rarely during the whole three hours was there any sign of human life—a few tiny villages huddled between the water and the forest were the only habitation, and a few toy boats were the only visible transportation. She was surely going to be a long way from anywhere in Iquitos.

She began to think of Edward again. The moody stranger had driven him from her mind since yesterday afternoon, but now Edward returned to her consciousness. Had she been right to crash out of his life on an impulse? She was already twenty-five years old, and Edward was the only man she had ever considered marrying. What were her chances of meeting anyone more suitable?

If she had not been stuck on this plane heading into the isolated Peruvian town that was her destination, she might at that moment have turned back from this crazy adventure. But to what? To the same routine of rulebook public health by day and family and friends telling her what to do during her off-duty hours.

Perhaps Dr. Morrison would be the kind of man she needed to direct her life for the next few weeks. In her mind's eye she saw him as a quiet, elderly, missionary-type physician who would be patient and orderly in his funny little world. With any luck he would leave her to run her own immunization program at his camp hospital or whatever it was. She would enjoy that, being on her own again, able to rediscover herself as an individual. That was what she really wanted, free expression of her personality, away from the badgering of others. She was a spunky girl, wasn't she? No way would she turn back now—she was going to plow into her new life with all the initiative and spirit she could find!

The plane circled, landed, and came to rest outside the airport building. Written on the back of her ticket was the address of her contact in Iquitos. La Casa del Corona, which she had translated as The Crown House, on the Avenida del Río, River Drive, was the place where she was to meet a certain Señor Muñoz, who would arrange accommodation overnight and put her in touch with Dr. Morrison.

As soon as she'd found her two suitcases at the baggage counter, she was happy to hand them over to a porter, who hurried ahead of her out to a waiting cab. At the mention of La Casa del Corona, the driver nodded approvingly "¡Sí señorita!" he said with an air of respect, and started off. She didn't even have to give the name of the street it was on.

The old taxi rattled its way into town, through what appeared to be the business and shopping section. All the signs were in Spanish, of course, but Carol picked out clean, modern banks, some smart clothing stores and shoe shops, and a quite respectable hotel. Iquitos had none of the humid decay of Manaus. Driving through the streets it was impossible to visualize that it was, like Manaus, totally cut off from the rest of the world except by plane or by boat. But this was Peru, not Brazil—somewhere on the flight they had crossed the border.

Creaking along, they came to an esplanade running beside the bank of the river. Carol read a sign, Avenida del Río. They passed some wharves and cranes and jetties for small craft, and then the avenida became a broad tree-lined avenue with huge houses set back in shady gardens. They entered one of these through a vast, rusty gate, now permanently open, traveled up a winding gravel drive through which moss and grass had grown in profusion, and skirted several stables and outhouses before drawing up opposite an enormous pillared portico. So this was La Casa del Corona, one of the most imposing private mansions that Carol had ever seen, even though it was a bit rundown and in need of new paint. She couldn't understand why she had been sent to this place, or who Señor Muñoz might be. It didn't look like the home of someone who devoted his life to a charitable organization that carried on good works among the natives of the jungle.

The taxi driver deposited her bags at the top of some well-worn stone steps and left Carol facing a pair of heavy mahogany doors with old brass handles the size of grapefruits. To one side an iron chain hung down. She pulled it, hoping that it was a bell. It was—a muffled clanging came from within.

She was about to try the bell again when one of the doors swung slowly open. A stooped old man with crinkly white hair peered out at her. He was wearing the black bow tie and maroon, braided monkey jacket of an old-time servant. He said nothing but just looked at her suspiciously.

"*Buenas tardes*," said Carol, using one of the few Spanish phrases she had learned. "Is Señor Muñoz at home?"

The servant opened the door barely wide enough for her to squeeze through with her bags. They were in a cavernous entrance hall, gloomily dark but refreshingly cool after the air outside. Dark paneling lined the walls, hung with portraits of Spanish noblemen in tight knickers and lace shirts; the ceiling was of intricately carved wood, supporting two silver and glass chandeliers, and tall leather chairs

19

stood like sentinels on the tiled floor. Carol felt dwarfed by the scale of everything.

The old man motioned to her to wait and shuffled off down a passage at the far end of the hall. Some moments later she heard heavy footsteps marching back down the same passage. They came round the corner. A big man stopped a few feet away, facing her. He looked less than thirty in spite of the telltale paunch under his conservative blue suit. He held himself erect. Slightly wavy black hair was brushed straight back from a low forehead, and his wide, full mouth was topped by a thick black mustache.

"Señor Muñoz?" said Carol. "I was told to come here . . ."

The man's big frame seemed to grow bigger. His chest broadened and neck stiffened as he stared down at her. Then he smiled and shook his head in disbelief. "You . . ." he said, "you are Nurse Baxter?"

"Yes, that's right," Carol replied brightly. "I'm glad I found the right place . . ."

Señor Muñoz moved a step closer. "Tell me, Señorita Baxter, do all American nurses resemble you?"

"Well, I guess some of us . . ."

"Then I must certainly go to America next time I fall ill. My recovery would be greatly speeded by the presence of such, er, delightful talent at my bedside."

Carol laughed uneasily. "I was told that you could put me on my way to the camp near here where Dr. Morrison works. He is expecting me today, so if you would be so kind . . ."

"My dear Miss Baxter"—the man relaxed more now and held out his hand to her—"It is not myself who has the charge of your arrangements, but my sister, Juanita, who lives with me in this house. She is very friendly with Ian Morrison—in fact one might almost say they are betrothed to be married—and because of that, you were asked to come here when you arrived."

"Oh, I see. Well then, if I could see your sister . . ."

"Naturally. I will take you to her. You can leave your luggage where it is. Come, Miss Baxter—your first name is Carol, is it not?—we will, I hope, be seeing a good deal of each other, so I will call you Carol and you will call me Ricardo. Follow me, Carol. Juanita is on the verandah."

He led the way across the echoing tile to the passage, through a richly decorated room with high plaster ceilings and gilt frescoes, and out through a paneled door with cut-glass handles into another passage.

"What an enormous house this is!" remarked Carol. "I somehow didn't expect to find anything like this in Iquitos."

"This house has been in my family for eight generations," answered Ricardo. "Juanita and I are the last of the line at present, so you will see that the time is fast approaching when I must think of marrying and producing an heir."

"He will be a lucky boy to inherit such a lovely home."

"Before I pass it on, I would like to restore it to its original grandeur. The outside particularly is showing signs of wear. And some of the furniture needs reupholstering . . ."

Ricardo now held open a glass door, and Carol passed through onto a shady stone terrace casually furnished with lawn chairs and wrought iron tables. Stretched out on one of the couches was a curvaceous young woman in a blue one-piece swimsuit and very large dark glasses. Her shining black hair was pulled back from her forehead and fell in a long ponytail over one shoulder. She looked up from the magazine she was reading as Carol and Ricardo came out onto the terrace. Then she pushed the glasses up onto her head and stared long and hard at Carol with dark, piercing eyes. Carol could almost feel the knife in the woman's gaze dissecting her body.

"Juanita, this is Carol Baxter. She has just arrived from the airport," announced Ricardo, as though he were expecting applause for a successful conjuring trick.

"We thought you would come earlier," Juanita said coldly. "In fact, we arranged to have some lunch kept for you."

"I'm sorry," said Carol, "my plane was late."

"Of course you're not to blame," said Ricardo soothingly. "Juanita should have known the planes are always late. Here, take this chair and join us in a cool drink. And let me take your jacket. It is warm out here." He insisted on helping Carol off with the jacket of the smart pantsuit she had traveled in and laid it gently on a chair. Then he poured her a tall glass of iced lemonade. She accepted his attentions with a smile, but Juanita looked on stonily.

"After this drink I must really move on," said Carol. "Juanita, Ricardo tells me you are going to put me in touch with Dr. Morrison. How can I find his camp?"

"The camp where Ian works is twenty miles upstream from here, in a very wild part of the jungle. It's not much, just a small primitive place belonging to an elderly naturalist called Henry Todd. He built it himself years ago and has lived there ever since, studying the birds and so on."

"That sounds fascinating," said Carol. "I'd love to live right out in the jungle . . ."

"Ian and I decided that it would be quite unsuitable for you to live there," Juanita cut in. "Having seen you, I am fully convinced that we were right. Ian unfortunately insists on living there—to be close to his patients as he calls them—but you will stay here in Iquitos and travel down each morning in the supply boat, which will also bring you back each afternoon. I have arranged accommodation for you in the town."

"Where have you put her?" asked Ricardo. "There isn't much except the Hotel Amazonas, and I'm sure the prices there would be beyond the reach of Carol's salary. I know that . . ."

"Ricardo, this is my business," snapped his sister. "Carol will stay at the Pension Maruja. It's . . ."

"The Maruja?" Ricardo sounded horrified. "That place? It's a dreadful, low-down . . . not at all the kind of place for a respectable, educated, attractive young lady such as Carol."

"There is nowhere else except the hotel, Ricardo. But then perhaps Miss Baxter wants to spend most of her money on living in comfort. If so, that's her business, not ours."

"Please call me Carol," she said with a friendly smile at

Juanita, who was still regarding her coldly. "No, I can't afford a smart hotel, even for only a week or two. Are you sure they couldn't find room for me at the camp? I don't mind roughing it. It would be rather exciting, and like the doctor, perhaps I should be near my patients."

"That's out of the question," replied Juanita. "Apart from anything else, it would be unseemly for you to live there virtually alone with Ian. I for one wouldn't hear of such a thing."

So that's it, thought Carol. She doesn't trust me out in the woods with her precious boyfriend. And maybe it was not such a good idea anyway. Days might be enough time with him as it was.

"Why don't I go and talk it over with the doctor myself?" said Carol. "If you're worried about anything, Juanita, let me assure you that my relationship with doctors I work for has always been strictly professional."

"Of course, of course," Ricardo cut in. "Juanita wasn't suggesting anything else, I'm sure. But I've visited the camp several times, and it wouldn't be at all suitable, my dear. Anyway, I have the solution. You will stay here with Juanita and me. We have eight spare bedrooms besides the one Ian uses . . ."

"They haven't been used for years," interrupted Juanita.

"What about Uncle Manuel's room? He was quite content there on his last visit from Lima. It's all cleaned up and tidy."

"I'd really rather discuss the whole thing with Dr. Morrison," said Carol. This wrangling was beginning to make her feel nervous. Surely the problem of her accommodation was one to be settled between her and her employer.

"You can't, I'm afraid," said Juanita. "He's away. That's why he left the matter in my hands."

"Away?" said Carol, surprised. "Where? And for how long?"

"He's collecting the measles vaccine for his silly program to immunize the Indians. It's just a waste of time, as I've told him many times, but he insists on trying to stop the poor wretched creatures from getting measles. It seems there have been a few local cases. Now, if he would just

23

forget this measles business and hurry up with the research study he's doing, he could be finished with his work here and on his way back to the States in no time. But he refuses to see the sense of that."

"I quite agree with him," said Carol. "Research is very important, but as a doctor he has to look after the health of the people as well. Measles vaccine is a hundred percent effective. One injection each and the epidemic would be wiped out. That's why he wants me here; I'm a public health nurse and used to carrying out mass immunization programs."

"You doctors and nurses don't understand these Indians," said Juanita scornfully. "I'll be glad when all this is over and Ian goes to New York—to the good, wealthy practice he'll have there instead of this nonsense. You see, I intend to go with him."

Carol decided not to argue the point any longer. If she was going to work with this Dr. Morrison, it would be better if she could get along with his fiancée or whatever she was—not that Juanita was making it very easy for her at the moment. "You didn't say when Dr. Morrison was coming back," she said.

"Maybe tomorrow, maybe the next day," Ricardo answered her question. "One never knows how long these things will take. So, meanwhile, my dear Carol, you are very welcome to stay with us here. I'm sure that once you have seen how pleasant it is, you will want to remain. We will charge you for your food and laundry, but that's all, because we already have the room . . ."

"But, Ricardo," Juanita tried again to dissuade her brother, "you know Ian stays here on weekends and sometimes on other nights too. Don't you think it would be a bit awkward if his little nurse were living here as well . . . ?"

"I'm sure Ian will be happy for Carol to be treated as one of the family. The house is near the jetty from which the camp boat leaves every day. On her off-duty time I will show her the local attractions. You and Ian will be left in peace, Juanita. I have decided. This is my house, and I will have no more argument."

Ricardo pressed an electric buzzer for the footman to take her to her room. Juanita sighed and picked up her magazine. Carol could see that she had no alternative but to accept the invitation.

Her room was huge with a four-poster bed and soft, downy pillows over crisp white sheets. It had an elaborate gilt-edged dressing table with a three-way mirror as well as a comfortable couch and armchair. A glass door led onto a private balcony overlooking the garden and the river. This luxury would be hard to give up for a sleazy boardinghouse in the town—or even for a bunk in a jungle camp.

After a long, hot bath she dried herself on the soft, enveloping towel that the maid, Teresa, brought her and dressed in her sleeveless linen again. It seemed wrong to wear anything more casual for her first dinner in these regal surroundings.

The meal was served formally by the aged footman who had let her into the house. Consommé first, then fluffy *tortillas* followed by *arroz con pollo*, a rice-chicken dish with crunchy lettuce and avocados that melted in one's mouth. Finally came sweet biscuits with strong Colombian coffee.

Juanita had changed into a frilly red and black dress and had let her hair hang loose in a way that emphasized her smouldering eyes—very much the noble, Andalusian señorita. Carol could see how poor Dr. Morrison had been smitten.

In spite of her flamenco-style appearance, Juanita spoke little during the meal, and Carol maintained a demeanor of quiet respect. Ricardo did nearly all the talking, mostly instructing Carol on the commercial prospects of this remote corner of Peru, local politics, and the hopeless backwardness of the natives.

Dinner ended at ten, and Carol was just about to excuse herself for bed when she heard a slight commotion coming from the entrance hall. The footman opened the door of the dining room and announced, "Señor Doctor Morrison."

Carol's new boss burst into the room. Juanita gave a little cry and ran to his side. Carol stood up, speechless

. . . Dr. Morrison was her companion in Manaus—the first person to sing her operatic arias and the first man ever to give her an orchid. "Hi there, Carol," he said casually. "So you got here."

Chapter 2

"I . . . you're Dr. Morrison?" Carol stammered.

"Large as life and twice as ugly," he assured her, although the expression certainly wasn't appropriate to the handsome, smiling face with crinkles around the eyes and graying temples that she saw before her.

Juanita stood back a pace from him, still firmly holding his arm. "Ian, you didn't tell me you knew Carol already. And you didn't tell us either, Carol, that you knew him. Why all the secrecy?" Her voice positively dripped with syrup—a very different Juanita from before.

"We only met yesterday," he answered her. "Bumped into each other on a bus in Manaus. I guessed who she was. What other Albany girl would be passing through Manaus on that particular day? She clinched it by admitting she was a nurse."

"Why didn't you say who you were, Dr. Morrison?" gasped Carol. "It . . ."

"Just for fun. You played cagey with me, so I played cagey with you. And my name's Ian."

A forced laugh from Juanita interrupted the looks that were passing between Ian and Carol, as if they were sharing a joke. "I'm sure you'll be wanting to go to bed now, Carol," she purred. "Ian and I have so much to talk about."

"I have a job for her first," said Ian. "In the hall there's an ice-packed box containing the antimeasles serum. Take the serum out and put it in the fridge in the kitchen."

Carol was surprised at the tone of authority with which he spoke. He was issuing commands already, there was no doubt about that. The smile on his face had vanished as soon as his mind was back on his job.

But then, equally abruptly, the smile was back as he added, "Sorry to put you to work so early, but we leave for the camp first thing tomorrow. That's a good girl now."

Carol wasn't sure she liked the patronizing tone any better than the brisk order, but she nodded and left the room, as Juanita led Ian away, her arm around his waist claiming his full attention.

She found a heavy metal box in the hall beside a small overnight bag and a rumpled raincoat. She wondered what was in the bag—there was hardly room for a change of clothes, and he was still wearing the T-shirt and pants he had on in Manaus. Obviously he was not a man who cared about his appearance very much—a shame, she thought, because he'd look marvelous dressed up . . . quickly she banished these irrelevant ideas from her head and lugged the box through into the kitchen.

The staff had gone off to bed, so she was alone when she started trying to open the strong metal container. The lid seemed to be fixed down by some sort of catch, and there was a pin through the catch, holding it firm. She got a knife from a drawer and pushed at the pin, but it wouldn't budge. She shoved at it until the knife began to bend, but nothing happened. In frustration she pushed back her hair from her face and stared at the wretched box, trying to see if there was another way to open it.

But her efforts were to no avail. There was only one thing to do—to go and disturb Dr. Morrison and get him to reveal the secrets of his annoying box. She hated to interrupt his tête-à-tête with Juanita—although she found a mischievous smile playing on her lips at the thought—but duty came first.

"Excuse me, Dr. Morrison," she said after a discreet

cough at the entrance to the dimly lit sitting room, "I'm afraid I can't get the container open."

Juanita's head appeared first over the back of the sofa. "Oh, for goodness' sake, I thought you'd gone to bed . . ."

"I had a job to do first, if you remember," said Carol icily as Ian's lanky frame also appeared.

"It's perfectly simple," he said, coming toward her. "I wouldn't have thought a smart girl like you, Carol, would be defeated by a little box."

"Tropical serum containers weren't included in my training," she retorted. "If you'll just show me how it works . . ."

"All right," he sighed. "I suppose there's no reason why you should be familiar with these containers. Come on then, I'll show you."

He marched into the kitchen. She followed, feeling guilty about disturbing him. Going over to the container, he flicked up a small lever Carol hadn't noticed, slid off the catch, and opened the box. The pin didn't have to come out after all.

She was bending over him watching the mystery being resolved when he straightened up quickly, bumping hard into her shoulder.

"I'm sorry," he said, taking hold of her elbow to steady her. "I didn't mean . . ." But instead of finishing the sentence he held firm onto her arm and fixed her pale hazel eyes with his gray ones. They remained still for a moment, his touch sending an inexplicable shiver through her body and causing her pulse to miss a beat.

He let her go and averted his gaze. "There now," he said, hardness again setting into his features, "do you think you can get the serum out by yourself?"

His sarcastic tone stung her. "I'll try," she answered shortly. "Thank you very much. I won't bother you again, Dr. Morrison."

"Good. I'll see you in the morning then. And, by the way, you should call me by my first name, which is Ian. It isn't as if there were any other doctors around—or other nurses either for that matter. We're the entire medical team up at the camp, Carol, so there's no need for formality. But there is need for a good deal of common sense. I'm sure I won't find you lacking in that."

"I hope not . . ." Carol started, but he stumped out of the room, leaving her to rub the elbow he had gripped and wonder why she had experienced that strange electric feeling when he had done so.

Pulling herself together, she quickly transferred the serum to the refrigerator and left the kitchen. Her path took her past the open door of the living room, where from the darkness of the dining room she could see Ian and Juanita at a small table now, she sipping a glass of wine while he munched on a late-night snack.

"She'll be all right when she gets used to things out here," he was saying. "At least I hope she will. As I told you, I just had two words with her on the tour bus."

Carol passed on quickly. Two words. Was that all they had had? What about the opera house? What about the voodoo waterfall? Above all, what about the orchid? Perhaps he had forgotten about those things already. Probably he had, now he was back in the arms of his "honey" and with all the important aspects of his work on his mind. Firmly she resolved to put their meeting in Manaus out of her mind too. From now on it was going to be a purely working relationship with Dr. Morrison, even if she did have to call him Ian . . .

On her way upstairs to her room she ran into Ricardo, resplendent in a green silk dressing gown, standing with one hand on the handle of the door next to Carol's own.

"I'm delighted you've agreed to stay here," he said. "As you saw, I have to put my foot down with my sister—she can be very difficult at times. But as the elder of us two, I have the last word in this house."

"It was very kind of you, Ricardo. I'm sure I'll be happy here." Carol started to move on down the passage, but he edged out to block her way.

"Not that Ian Morrison isn't difficult, too, in his own way. They're good for each other, I say. Anyway, I hope he doesn't give you too bad a time, Carol. If there's anything I can do . . ."

"I find him quite charming," she cut in tersely. "I'm

looking forward to working with him. Now, if you'll excuse me . . ."

Ricardo moved aside to let her pass. "If you want, er, anything in the night, my room is this one," he said with a knowing smile. "Don't hesitate to waken me."

"Thank you, but I'm quite certain I won't want anything, tonight or any other night. I sleep very soundly."

"Yes . . . yes, of course," Ricardo nodded. "I just thought I'd let you know where I am."

"Good night, Ricardo," said Carol, and went on into her room. She was happy to see there was a strong bolt on the door.

Teresa had turned down her bed since she had changed for dinner and had laid out her filmy chiffon nightie. Carol slipped quickly out of her dress and put on the nightie and its matching negligee. Then she went out onto the balcony. Below lay the moonlit garden and the river beyond. In the distance she could hear frogs croaking and some night bird repeating its insistent call.

Downstairs the soft light from the sitting room faintly illuminated the terrace where she had sat that afternoon. Music filtered up to her—she nearly laughed when she recognized it as opera. Was it *Madame Butterfly*? She couldn't remember. Somehow she had never thought of opera as music to make love by—presumably that was what was going on down there between Dr. Morrison and his "honey"—although love was usually the theme of operas, the singing seemed too hearty somehow.

Putting the imagined scene downstairs out of her mind, she began to wonder whether it was going to be hard to work with Dr. Ian Morrison. Or was it going to be more like working *for* him? As a nurse she was certainly used to taking directions from doctors, but barked out orders and heavy sarcasm was something she had never had to put up with.

Was she really looking forward to it, as she had so confidently assured Ricardo? Well, in a way she was . . . looking forward to it immensely. The idea of helping all those poor Indians alongside such an obviously dedicated person was what she had come to Peru for. And the idea of being close to him, talking with him, alone with him in the jungle for day after day . . . that idea quickened her pulse and brought a smile of satisfaction to her lips. And she needn't be concerned that he might try to take advantage of their close relationship. Juanita was looking after that department of his life. She was glad—it was still too soon after Edward.

Next morning she was determined to put on her best air of brisk efficiency. She would keep her wits constantly about her, so as to forestall any possibility of giving Dr. Morrison an opportunity to criticize her or find her inadequate. She put on the crisp white drip-dry nurse's uniform she had brought with her and the new white shoes and stockings and pinned her pert little nurse's cap on top of the neat chignon into which she had tied her auburn hair. She went downstairs feeling ready for anything.

Anything, that was, but what greeted her. Juanita, Ricardo, and Ian were at the breakfast table. They all stopped eating and looked up when Carol made her entrance.

"Good morning!" she said, smiling cheerfully all around. "Here we are all ready for the day's work."

The brother and sister stared at her blankly, so she let her smile fall on Ian. But it froze on her face when his only reaction was to turn down the corners of his mouth and shake his head resignedly from side to side.

Then Juanita burst into uncontrollable giggles. Covering her mouth with one hand she pointed at Carol with the other, the phrases, "Oh no! Oh no! Look at her!" coming out distorted with laughter.

Carol could have sunk through the floor. Tears, partly of anger, partly of mortification, welled up. But she stood her ground, glaring at her hostess. "Perhaps you'll be so kind as to tell me what's funny," she said, tremor breaking through her icy tone.

Juanita's convulsions continued until Ricardo told her sharply to cut it out. He himself sat there looking acutely embarrassed.

It was left to Ian to explain the humor of the situation. He did so with a sigh, gesturing to an empty chair at the table. "Come and sit down, Carol, and have some breakfast. And don't worry, you look fine, just fine—for a nice, well-scrubbed, six-hundred-bed hospital."

"And what's so wrong with that, may I ask?" She felt the back of her neck prickling at the slight sneer in his voice. "I happen to have worked . . ."

"I know you have, Nurse Nancy. And so have I. But that's not at all what we have at the camp. We have a thatched roof, rough wooden floors, and hammocks for beds. And we have mud, lots of mud, and mosquitoes. And not even any electricity. Your legs and arms would get eaten alive in that outfit. Foot-worms would find their way over the top of your shoes whenever you had to wade in the mud, and you would become very ill with bilharziasis. And your pretty white dress would become spattered and dirty within an hour."

"And a monkey would pinch her little white hat!" added Juanita, relapsing into giggles again.

"There's no need to be cruel to the poor girl," said Ian in mild rebuke to Juanita, one that Ricardo strongly echoed.

Carol sat down feeling sheepish, but she had to admit that the scene that had been painted for her did have its amusing side. Somehow she had never thought of working as a nurse in anything but a nurse's uniform. Oh, what had possessed her to make such a fool of herself in front of Ian Morrison!

Instinct told her that the quickest way to drive away the nasty smirk that still hovered on Juanita's lips was to accept her foolish mistake and pass it off lightly. "Yes, I suppose it was kind of dumb of me to dress like this. I knew what the camp would be like—and I'm quite prepeared for it—but for some reason I never thought . . . force of habit made me . . ." Her explanation faded out lamely.

Ian put down his cup of coffee. "Well, I'm afraid your lack of intelligent forethought will force me to change my plans a bit." The sympathetic look he had had for Carol's discomfiture was now replaced by a frown. "But it can't be helped. I'll take you into town this morning to get some sensible clothes for the kind of work you'll be doing. We'll leave for the camp as soon as we can after that. Pity, I'd wanted to get cracking on the immunization today . . ."

Ricardo cut in to offer to buy Carol some appropriate clothes, so as not to delay Ian's departure to the camp. He also apologized for his sister's unkind and unseemly behavior.

"I think Carol's enough of a sport to take a little good-natured ribbing. Aren't you, Carol?" A smile broke out on his handsome features, and Carol felt a warm flush creep into her cheeks at this rare word of appreciation. She nodded as he went on, "And I wouldn't trust you to get the right things for her, Ricardo. You'd have her turned out looking like a movie star in a Hollywood production of jungle life—something quite unsuitable. No, I'll take her myself to make sure she gets something really practical, however unbecoming it may be."

Upstairs after breakfast Carol deliberated on what to put on to go shopping with Ian. She was tempted to wear the strapless blue top and midriff he had admired in Manaus, especially as she was to be condemned to something "unbecoming" all the time she was with him from now on. Finally she decided not to risk further scorn and pulled on a pair of jeans and a simple striped cotton shirt.

"Aren't you ever coming?" She heard Ian's voice calling from downstairs. Slipping her feet into some sandals, she hurried down to meet him. He was, she had noted at breakfast, in jeans, sandals, and a loose khaki shirt himself, so he could have no cause for complaint about her attire now. "Ah, that's better," he said when he saw her. "We only need the protective stuff when we go out into the bush. What you've got on will do fine for the camp." Thank goodness, she thought, I've done something right at last.

Carol climbed into her side of the jeep he kept parked around the back of the house. Ian soon pulled up outside a shop called Almacén de Expediciónes. He was out of the jeep and through the door before she had even manipulated the handle to let herself out. He was waiting impatiently, holding the door for her, when she came up to him. "Sorry, I . . ." she began, but he was already pouring out a flood of Spanish at the lady who ran the shop.

The lady inclined her head understandingly and led Carol into a small changing room. Then she reappeared with a tan-colored safari suit of light, closely woven material. The bottoms of the pants were elasticized to fit snugly around the ankles, and the sleeves were the same. The jacket had a belt and deep pockets at the sides and on the chest. It certainly looked efficient if not very glamorous.

She pulled on the pants, but the seat bagged horribly, and she could stuff both hands inside the waist. *"Demasiado grande,"* she said to the lady, who shrugged her shoulders helplessly and indicated the gentleman outside.

"El señor dice . . . cómodo . . ." said the lady, but Carol put a finger to her lips conspiratorially and whispered for her to bring a smaller size. When it came she found the seat fitted snugly, and the jacket, with the belt tightened, was tight enough to allow her bosom to protrude fetchingly under the breast pockets.

She padded out in her socks to meet Ian's inspection and was delighted to see a grin of approval cross his face. "With your figure you can even make a bush jacket look attractive," he said, more relaxed than he had been all morning.

"Are you sure it's comfortable?" he asked, the worried look coming back. "You're going to have to scramble through all kinds of rough country in that outfit."

"Perfect," she smiled back. "I could climb the Andes in it, if you want me to."

"All right then, now the boots. What size are your dainty little feet?"

Actually Carol had always thought her feet a little too large for beauty, but Ian translated her size eight into the South American equivalent, and the pair brought by the shop lady fitted her nicely. The firm leather uppers laced over the elastic on her pants—no marauding insect could ever get past that barrier—and the soles were so strong that she felt she could tramp for miles in them. Ian nodded approvingly as she stomped round the floor.

"Now for the crowning glory," he said, striding over to

a row of hats on a shelf. After assessing the size of her head with a quizzical twinkle in his gray eyes that made her wilt a little, he brought over a brown canvas topee with a veil of mosquito netting hanging down from the brim.

He set it on her head, pushed it back a little, and moved away to admire the effect. She smiled, her even row of white teeth gleaming, at his obvious pleasure at his handiwork. "You can wear the net hanging down like that," he said, "or if you think it's going to get snagged on branches that way, you can tuck it in like this." He came close up to her now, so close that she could feel his breath on her cheek, and with gentle fingers methodically tucked the netting into her collar all the way around. His touch set her heart pounding in a way she could neither understand nor control, and she stood there motionless as he worked the delicate material against the skin of her neck.

By the time he had finished she felt sure his breath was coming a little faster too. At last he stood back, his eyes crinkled with delight, and met her steady gaze for what seemed like endless minutes.

"Yes, that does it fine," he said, his brisk tone snapping her back into reality. "You can get out of your fancy dress now. We've got work to do today, and it's late."

Desperate not to offend him again, Carol stripped off the safari suit as quickly as she could and emerged from the changing room in her jeans and shirt to find Ian paying the shop lady. "I've got the money for these things," she said. "It was my fault not getting them before I came down here."

"No, that's all right," he answered without looking up, "You couldn't really be expected to know. I'll put in for the cost as a clothing allowance. They'll probably pay me back."

"Be sure to let me know if they don't," she said earnestly. "I should pay for my stupidity."

"We'll see how stupid you are later in the day, if we can ever get out of this town and start work."

They sped back to the Muñoz villa in the jeep, and Ian

sent Carol to collect the serum from the refrigerator while he picked up a few things of his own.

Juanita came to the front door to see them off. Hanging onto Ian's arm until the last moment, she held up her mouth to be kissed, but Carol noted with satisfaction that all she received was a peck on the cheek. Carol suffered no illusions, however, that Juanita had been wooed with only a simple kiss or two last night after everyone else had gone to bed.

"I'll see you this evening," Carol waved from her seat in the jeep, but Juanita didn't seem to hear. She whispered something in Ian's ear, which made him smile momentarily, and released him from her grasp. He leapt into the driver's seat, and they set off down the drive in a cloud of dust. Carol stole a sideways glance at his face, but it revealed only a stony concentration on the road ahead.

"Usually I walk from the house to the jetty," he said. "It's not more than a half a mile, but we're in a hurry today. You can walk back when the boat brings you down here again tonight."

"Okay."

"Do you like walking, Carol?"

"Yes, but I like biking better. You get around so much faster. I used to bike a lot in Albany and around New York State."

"Ah, yes, New York . . ." he said thoughtfully, "I guess I'm going to have to go back there soon."

Carol was longing to ask him about his life and ambitions, but he changed the subject abruptly. "And what else do you like, Carol?"

"Well, I can tell you what I don't like," she smiled at the reminiscence that came to mind. "I don't like opera—especially if someone tells me I should like it."

"Yes . . . that reminds me," he said, frowning slightly. "I'd prefer that you forgot that little episode, if you don't mind."

"Oh, it was rather fun. I don't hold it against you, Ian. You weren't a big bore about it like someone else I know."

"No, it's not that. It's just . . . well, I didn't know who

you were then, remember. And not until we were almost at the end of the bus trip either. If I had known . . ."

"You'd not have flirted with me. Is that it?"

"I felt sure you'd understand. Thank you." He took his eyes off the road for a minute to give her a look she hadn't expected to see on those strong, confident features. An appeal almost. He was ashamed of their brief, harmless relationship in Manaus. And afraid that Juanita might find out. All right, she thought, I won't let him down.

"So you don't like mixing business and pleasure, eh?" She watched him carefully as she said it.

"Something like that. Well, here we are at the jetty. I'm glad to see the boat's still waiting." The jaunty, matter-of-fact manner had returned. Carol sighed imperceptibly.

Antonio, the driver of the boat, was asleep on the cushions, but awoke immediately on Ian's command. Moments later they were curving away from the jetty into the mainstream of the great river. Even here, two thousand miles from the sea, the marshland on the far bank looked far away, and Carol noticed an ocean-going cargo ship unloading at the wharves nearer the city. Now that she was really heading into the unknown some of Ian's confidence rubbed off onto her. She felt exhilarated by the wind in her hair and by his presence beside her in the stern of the boat as it skimmed over the water, spreading a frothing wake behind it.

"I better brief you about the camp on the way down," he shouted into her ear over the roar of the engine. "It'll save time when we get there, as I want us both to start work right away. There are about a thousand Indians living within easy reach of the camp, and we'll inoculate them first as that's where all the measles cases have been so far. Then there's another thousand we can get to by canoe. We'll do them later, hopefully before the epidemic spreads to them."

When she turned her head to nod her understanding, his face was so close that she could see every hair of his bushy eyebrows and the sparkle of excitement in his eyes. She knew the excitement was over his medical program—

she shared his keenness but she also savored the anticipation of working with him as a man.

"The only thing I don't understand is why you are going to all this trouble over a few cases of measles. In the States we don't carry out a mass immunization unless there's a really serious outbreak, and then we only give it to the children."

"I suppose they didn't teach you about that in your nursing course either," he said, and she was dismayed to see his forehead wrinkle in another frown. "Measles is a very different problem in a community of primitive Indians who have never been exposed to it before. It can wipe out whole tribes in a matter of weeks, children and adults alike. That's why it's so important to give them all protection as soon as the first few cases appear. I only hope we're in time with the Yaguas."

"The who?"

"The Yagua Indians. They're the people who live all around here. The men wear long grass skirts and paint their faces red, which is why the early Spanish conquerors thought they were fighting women and reported that they had encountered a race of female warriors, which they called the Amazons."

"They've survived," laughed Carol, remembering her days in training. "In the form of hospital matrons and head ward nurses."

Ian grinned back. "I can't see you ever becoming a tyrannical head nurse. You're much too . . ." Carol waited anxiously for him to say what she was, but he never finished the sentence. Instead he changed the subject back to the camp.

He told her there were only two other people working there apart from the cook and the girl who cleaned the place. One was old Dr. Todd, the eccentric naturalist who first built it years ago and had lived there ever since, although everyone told him he should retire to more comfortable quarters at his age. "I'm worried about Henry," said Ian. "I've examined him, and his heart isn't too strong, but he refuses to move—says the jungle has been his life and will be his death, too. He knows everything there is to know about the plants and animals. You'll like him."

"I'm sure I will," said Carol. "Who's the other person working at the camp?"

"An Indian called Jutai. He's Henry Todd's assistant really, but since I arrived he's been very useful to me, too. He's the local witch doctor of the village, and held in great respect by the others. But fortunately Henry has taught him to accept many of our ways of doing things, including modern medicine. It's because of Jutai's influence that I've been able to accomplish as much as I have for the people. They let me examine their babies as much as I like for my research study, and you'll find they accept our immunization needles without any qualms. Jutai makes it all much easier."

"I'm glad to hear that," said Carol. "I wouldn't like to have to wrestle with some hefty Indian trying to stick a needle into him."

Ian grimaced. "You'd never succeed anyway. They're much too strong." His mouth grew stern again. "But seriously, Carol, you must always remember that these people are our friends and that you mustn't antagonize them in any way."

"I was only joking," she declared, but inside it worried her that he had felt the need to warn her after such an innocent remark.

They sat in silence for a while after that as the boat raced on up the river. Carol saw a school of porpoises flopping in and out of the water, and overhead some huge birds circled, looking for prey. Iquitos was left far behind now, and the only signs of human life were occasional thatched huts built on stilts at the water's edge and rafts being poled along in the shallows carrying boxes and piles of sacks.

Ian had turned away from her, squinting into the sun as he peered ahead, anxious, no doubt, to get back as soon as possible to the camp where his heart lay—that part of it, at least, which was not languishing in a sundress or brushing her silky black hair until it shone, awaiting his return. Carol relished the thought that Juanita would have to wait

39

for several days, while she herself would be with him every day, a part of his working routine. That was something Juanita could never be, even after the betrothal that Ricardo had hinted at had blossomed into marriage.

Suddenly Ian spoke to her again. Eagerly she leaned forward to listen. "Jutai has a daughter," he said, his eyes sparkling with enthusiasm. "She's eleven years old and her name is Maria Luisa, although I call her Chicua, which is Spanish for cuckoo. She's a very bright little girl who learned English as a baby from Henry Todd. Because she's so bright she goes to the best convent school in Iquitos and only comes back to the camp on Sundays, so I don't see as much of her as I would like. But I can put up with that because she's getting the education she deserves. She's determined to be a doctor, Carol. What do you think of that?"

"That's very good. I hope she makes it. I suppose you put the idea into her head."

"Yes, I guess I did to some extent. But Jutai is all for it, too. He has remarkable insight considering he owes his prestige to the mumbo jumbo business of witch doctoring."

"Is that all mumbo jumbo?"

"All except for the use of a few herbs for medicinal treatment. Though Henry doesn't agree—he's lived surrounded by it for so long. You know, if Chicua graduates as a doctor, she'll be the first Yagua girl ever to do so. Isn't that something? I'll be proud to have gotten her started."

"You like your women to be intelligent, don't you, Ian?"

"Yes, I do . . . for working purposes, anyway. For other purposes, well, I find the lively, poised, beautiful type gives me the relaxation I need."

Juanita all over, thought Carol. Perhaps she is right for him after all. Anyway, what business is it of mine?

The driver suddenly cut the motor, and the boat moved in a slow semicircle toward the swampy left bank. As it came nearer, Carol could see a narrow gap in the land, the mouth of a creek leading into the river. They edged closer and closer to the entrance, and a few minutes later were sliding along almost touching a clump of tall, luxuri-ant-looking reeds. Simply out of curiosity she reached out and took hold of one particularly succulent reed—then im-mediately wished she hadn't, because the motion of the boat caused it to run through her hand, cutting it. Drops of blood began dripping onto the deck.

Although the wound was only slight, Carol felt that she should wash it and plunged her hand over the side into the warm water. Now she had cause to regret this move also, because her arm was firmly taken from behind and lifted out. Blood, pink with water, continued to drip.

"Carol, Carol, Carol!" Consternation mixed with exas-peration clouded his expression. "Don't you know that you must never, never wash a bleeding wound in this river water?" He shook his head sadly as though she had in some lamentable way failed him.

"N-no . . . Why not?" she replied, staring miserably at her hand.

"Because of the piranhas, of course. They could have all the flesh off your hand in seconds. They're all through these creeks, and one ounce of blood is enough to bring dozens of them rushing to the spot."

"Piranhas?" Carol asked weakly. "What are they?"

"You never heard of piranhas?" he said incredulously. "They're tropical fish that attack humans the moment they sense blood around."

Carol was again distressed that this otherwise marvelous man could be so unreasonable. "You seem to forget that my education was in the States, not in the tropics. I can't learn everything in a single day." She felt at a disad-vantage with Ian holding her wrist in his firm grip, the blood still oozing gently out of the cut, but she had the courage to add, "And you didn't seem to mind that I didn't know about Brazil nuts and voodoo . . . and or-chids in Manaus."

He let her hand drop and gazed into her eyes, that look of vulnerability again flashing across his face. "I thought you promised to forget all about Manaus," he said softly.

"It's not so easy," she replied, averting her eyes from his unnerving stare of accusation. "But I'll . . . I'll try . . ."

"How did you cut it anyway?" He picked up her hand again, gently professional this time, and examined the wound.

"On those reeds if you want to know. And don't tell me that I should have known better than to touch them. In New York State the reeds don't grow razor-sharp." She didn't disguise her annoyance.

His mouth broke into an unexpected smile. "I know. I come from there, too. I'll put a bandage on your hand as soon as we get ashore. Here, wrap this clean handkerchief around it for now."

As she took his handkerchief and pressed it to her hand, his tenderness brought that odd, disquieting sensation over her. After her outburst and his surprisingly sympathetic reaction, she didn't know whether she wanted to laugh or cry. Fortunately she was able to control herself from doing either, as by now the boat was easing up to a landing stage made of rough, unhewn logs on which a small, dark man was waving them a friendly greeting.

"Hello, Jutai," called Ian, throwing ashore a line for the man to secure to a bollard. The jetty was built on pilings that supported it eight feet above the water level, and Carol could see that the buildings behind it were similarly stuck up in the air. "When the floods come next month the water will rise almost to the level of the camp," Ian told her. "For now we have to go up and down this ladder." He had already started up it, carrying the serum container, and she followed, clutching her parcel of bush clothes.

Ian waited at the top for her to scramble up after him, but made no effort to assist her. At last she was able to heave the parcel onto the wooden planks and hoist herself in ungainly fashion up beside it. She got up off her knees and stood there, dusting off her jeans and pushing back a lock of hair that had fallen over her face. "So this is it," she said, looking around at the raised platform on which the camp was built. Windowless thatched huts surrounded it, nestled into the impenetrable forest. The trees intertwined many feet overhead, so that the jungle was sunless and cool compared to the heat of Iquitos and the river.

"Jutai, this is Nurse Baxter, whom I told you about. Carol, this is Jutai," said Ian, making the introduction.

"Welcome, nurse," said Jutai, taking Carol's hand with a little bow. "It is very good that you have come. Perhaps now the doctor will not have so much hard work to do."

"Nurse Baxter is just here to help with the immunization program," Ian explained. "I'll still have my study and other medical work to do. Tell me, Jutai, have there been any fresh cases of measles in the few days I've been away?"

"I am happy that only two," beamed Jutai. "And they are in families already affected."

"That *is* good news. If we inoculate the neighbors of those families this afternoon, maybe we'll have the problem licked."

"Very well, doctor. I will have them come down here. Do you wish to rest first after your journey? Perhaps the lady . . ."

"Rest? Since when have you known Dr. Morrison to want to rest when there's work to be done?" A gaunt, wiry old gentleman with a white beard and a shock of white hair had joined them while they were talking. He must have been well over seventy.

"Ah, Henry!" said Ian, bringing the newcomer into the group. "I'd like you to meet Carol Baxter. Carol, meet Henry Todd. It's through his hospitality that we're here at all."

"Delighted to have you here, young lady. I'm afraid this place is not at all what you're used to, but we'll try to make things comfortable for you. Will she be living here, Ian?"

"No, it's not really necessary. She's going to stay with the Muñozes and and come down each day on the boat."

"Ah . . . Ricardo Muñoz will entertain her, no doubt."

"I'm here to work, not to be entertained, Mr. Todd," said Carol, with a mischievous glance at Ian.

"That's true," Ian snapped. "And Henry is Dr. Todd, not Mr. Todd. He's not a medical doctor, but he does have a doctorate in biology. Though I expect he'd rather you called him Henry."

"Of course," nodded the biologist. "I'm not so old that I don't enjoy being on familiar terms with pretty young ladies."

"Now, Henry, don't flatter her, or it'll go to her head, and she'll spend half her time titivating instead of getting on with the job." Ian looked faintly annoyed.

Not that you'd notice the results if I did, thought Carol. Aloud she said, "Thank you, Henry. I appreciate the compliment."

"Well, let's get cracking!" said Ian impatiently. "We'll split up into two teams. Jutai, set up a table on the jetty here for me to work from, will you, and we'll put Carol on the verandah over there with Henry to give her a hand. The people don't know her yet, and you could reassure them, Henry, if you don't mind."

"It would be a pleasure," said the old man with a twinkle in his eye. "Though I'm sure Carol has only to smile at them and she could stick as many needles into them as she likes."

"Henry, please!" remonstrated Ian. "All right, Jutai, take the canoe to the village and bring the first batch over. I'll show Carol the equipment and put a bandage on her finger."

Ian strode away down the jetty, Carol half-running to keep up with his long legs. In the room that he used as a medical office, he pulled out two sterilizers operated by butane gas, some syringes and hypodermic needles, and a box of alcohol swabs. Within minutes he had dressed her wound and set up her worktable where the camp dwellers sat for their meals. Then he went off to lay out his own equipment twenty yards away on the jetty. She watched him busily lighting the sterilizer and preparing for the injections with as much earnest concentration as a small boy playing with his model trains.

"He's doing some wonderful work here," remarked Henry as they waited for the first patients to arrive. "It's been breaking my heart for years to see so many of the Yaguas become ill so needlessly, but since Ian arrived . . . He's a brilliant doctor."

"What brought him here in the first place?" asked Carol.

"He's doing a medical study on the Indians. It will bring him an international reputation when it's finished. Then he'll go. It's a waste for him to be stuck away in a hole like this . . . !"

"It's not a hole, Henry. It's beautiful. I love it. I can't think how you managed to build it all by yourself way out here in the jungle."

"It took a long time, my dear. But I'm glad you like it. I do too." He smiled at her wisely, showing the gaps in his teeth, which had resulted from years of personal neglect. "Yes, we'll miss Ian when he's gone. But one day perhaps the Yaguas will have their own doctor here—did he tell you about Chicua?"

"Yes, he did. He seems very fond of the child."

"It's a marvelous thing he's done, setting up a trust fund for her with his own money to finance her education all through medical school."

"I didn't know he'd done that," said Carol, surprised. "Where did he get the money from? Medical school's expensive."

"Oh, didn't you know? Ian's a rich man. His father left him a small fortune to establish a Tropical Diseases Institute in New York. He finished his specialist training in Houston a few months ago and came down here to do his study and help the Indians at the same time. He's due to finish his study in a week or two and has to go straight to New York City to open the institute when he leaves here. He'll be a famous man before he's through."

Carol nodded thoughtfully. "How old is he, do you know?"

"About thirty-five. He had a successful practice in the States before he went into tropical medicine. Ah, here come your first patients."

Jutai was approaching, leading a straggle of Indians, all of them barefoot, some dressed in grass skirts and some with grass wigs on their heads surmounted with a crown of gaily colored feathers. Carol tried not to laugh when she saw that these were men—they must indeed have looked like fierce, powerful women to the early explorers.

They all obviously knew Henry well, and, talking to

them in their own language, he had no trouble at all persuading each in turn to offer her their arms for injection. Measuring the dose of serum according to the estimated weight of the patient, she deftly inoculated each one as the line moved past. Afterward the first to receive the serum proudly showed their tiny pin pricks to those who were waiting. Carol felt happy that these, at least, would not succumb to the deadly measles.

After a while she had used up her supply of sterile needles and was forced to delay the proceedings until they had all been boiled up again. She noticed that Ian, at his table on the jetty, was still working away at great speed—she assumed that he had a bigger supply of needles than she did.

While waiting for the sterilizer she and Henry continued their chat. "What do you know about the Muñozes, Henry?" she asked.

"Only that they're one of the oldest families in Iquitos," he replied. "But I hear that they've lost most of their wealth. I believe Ricardo made some bad investments, and taxes have taken the rest. I don't interest myself much in the local gossip—you'll know more about them than I do after you've been there for a few days."

"Did you know Ian is supposed to be getting engaged to Juanita Muñoz?"

"I didn't indeed. But then he seldom discusses his private life with me. Nevertheless, I'm surprised. I would have thought . . ."

Carol never had the chance to ask Henry the reason for his surprise, because Ian himself was now bearing down on them with that familiar look of unhappiness marring his features.

"Oh Carol, for heaven's sake!" he growled. "Why aren't you working? There's a whole line of people waiting, and you . . ."

"How can I work when I've run out of sterilized needles?" she retorted in a voice that matched his. "They'll be boiled up again in a minute, and then we can carry on."

"You really aren't very bright today, are you?" he threw

46

back. "If you get each needle back in the sterilizer as soon as you've used it, it'll be ready for use again by the time you've used the others. That way you won't ever run out of clean ones and have to stop work."

"I've never worked in a place before where there's a short supply of needles," she said haughtily, horribly aware that she was on the defensive. She should have counted the needles before she started and thought of Ian's method herself. Oh, why did she have to lay herself open to another of his criticisms!

"I don't know, Carol," he said, running his fingers through his dark curly hair. "I don't know if you're the sort of nurse I was looking for when I placed that advertisement. You just don't seem to be able to adapt . . ." His mouth began to twitch in something like rage.

Carol flared up. "If you weren't so picky all the time . . . If you just had a little more patience . . ."

"Patience?" his eyebrows shot up. "I can tell you, my patience with *you* is just about exhausted." He stalked off back to his table.

Henry was looking shocked. "I'm sorry to see that, my dear," he said. "I've never seen Ian so upset. It reminds me of the physical chastisement the young Yagua men give to a girl they are thinking of marrying. If she stands up to it without breaking, he takes her as his bride. But if she cracks up, the man goes looking for someone else."

Carol grinned in spite of her angry flush. "And how does the girl calm her man down after the wedding? Or does he go on beating her?"

"Oh no," said Henry. "On her wedding night she gives him a love potion that makes him sweet and docile. Jutai makes a particularly effective one. He charges a lot for it, too."

"If Ian's following the Yagua custom, I'm sorry for Juanita. If he treats *me* this way, think what he must do to *her*. She'll need to buy a huge dose of love potion for her wedding night, poor girl!"

Chapter 3

By late afternoon the queue of patients whom Jutai had organized had come to an end. Wearily Carol laid down her syringe and saw that Ian had finished too and was putting away his equipment. She did the same, scrupulously tidy to avoid further criticism. She met him coming out of the medical office and noted that the look of rage had gone from his eyes, leaving them curiously wistful.

"Jutai has got a glass of lemonade for us," he said without expression. "On the verandah. Come out when you're ready."

When she got there she found Ian sprawled on a deck chair, sipping from his glass. She helped herself from the jug and sat in another chair. No words passed between them.

Presently Jutai bustled up and handed Ian a necklace that seemed to be made of polished stones of different sizes and shapes. It was attractive, and definitely unusual.

Ian immediately perked up, examining the necklace minutely. "Oh, they finished it!" he exclaimed. "That's great. I know she'll love it."

"You see, doctor," Jutai beamed, pointing out the stones. "They found an agate and an opal as you requested."

"So they did. It's really beautiful. You know, I think I'll take it down to her this afternoon and stay the night. It's a good excuse to see my honey again, and Antonio can bring me back early in the morning." He gave Carol a curt nod. "I'll come down with you then. We better leave in five minutes."

"Yes, *sir*," Carol snapped back. Her tone and form of

address produced a momentary look of horror on his face—to Carol's satisfaction.

She was already in the boat when Ian climbed down the ladder and joined her. But she was careful not to acknowledge his arrival, keeping her eyes fixed in the opposite direction, focused on a disused termites' nest high in a tree, which a family of parrots had adopted as their home.

Antonio started the engine, and they set off down the river. This time neither of them made any attempt at conversation, each engrossed in his own thoughts. To her annoyance she found herself wondering what he was thinking—why should she care anyway?—as for herself, all she knew was that she couldn't bear to go on making a fool of herself any longer. It was too humiliating in front of him. Somehow she seemed doomed to make stupid little errors while working for the one man whose approval she had most wanted all her life. She would take the next plane out of Iquitos even if it meant going back to Albany with her tail between her legs. She might even go back to Edward. He was conceited, possessive, and rude, but at least he showed her some respect as a woman.

As soon as the boat touched the dock in Iquitos, Carol jumped out and started heading briskly toward the Muñoz villa. She walked determinedly, but not too fast, just in case . . .

"Carol!" Ian was calling after her. "Come on, I'll give you a ride."

She stopped. Would she? Dare she? Yes, some uncontrollable force made her turn and return slowly to the jeep. She climbed in and sat beside him but couldn't bring herself to look in his direction. She struggled to keep her features blank and impassive, hiding the welter of mixed emotions that churned inside her.

She sensed that he was looking at her now. What was she going to do if he apologized?

After a full minute's silence, he said, "I suppose you're thinking of leaving after what I said to you this afternoon."

"I certainly am. Isn't that what you wanted?"

"I was hasty. I don't really want you to go. Please

reconsider." He sounded sincere, but did that make any difference? No apology—one was hardly called for—but the use of the word "please" was something new in the way he spoke to her. Perhaps that augured well for the future.

"I don't think I can be of any further use to you."

"Oh, but you can, you know. And to the Indians. After all, you have done mass immunizations before, and I don't know how I could . . . how long it would take to get a . . . a replacement."

Did she owe the Indians anything? What about her duty as a nurse apart from her own feelings? "I'll think about it," she said, knowing already what her decision was going to be and thankful that the Indians had saved her from having to make it on a personal basis.

"Thank you," he said simply.

As he did so, he put a hand on her knee and squeezed it gently. It was a patronizing gesture, but all the same the pressure of his hand drove all reason out of her mind. All she wanted to do now was to please him, to earn his commendation.

She looked at him. His deep eyes were boring into hers with an intensity that quickened her pulse and made her feel faint. She looked away quickly. "All right, I'll stay. But it's only because I don't want to go back to Albany just yet. That and the Indians, of course."

"I see," he said. "I wondered why you took the job out here. Were you getting away from some man?"

"Yes. I broke off an engagement on Christmas Day."

"Christmas Day? Then you must have had a very good reason. What was he like?"

"Too damn like you in many ways!" The words were out before she could stop them, but he laughed, and she couldn't help looking at him again and laughing too. The rift was healed. Carol couldn't understand how he had healed it so easily.

A few minutes later Ian guided the jeep up the drive of the Muñoz villa and stopped. "I'll see you for dinner," he said, and drove off again.

Now where's he going, Carol wondered. To get her another present? You'd have thought a necklace of semiprecious stones would be enough. It's incredible how Juanita has managed to snare him so thoroughly, considering what a self-disciplined, self-reliant, self-contained person he is. It could only be the physical attraction she exuded so blatantly and which he himself had admitted to needing in his off-duty hours.

She let herself in through the massive front door and was about to go to her room for a bath and change, when Ricardo caught her. "Good, you're back," he said warmly. "I was afraid that slave driver would keep you working up there half the night."

"As a matter of fact he's come back himself," she replied. "It seems he finds it hard to stay way from your sister for very long."

"Ah yes, love is a powerful magnet!" said Ricardo, spreading his hands wide in an all-embracing gesture. "I'm sure that many men have traveled farther to be with *you*. It is surprising that you haven't yet been swept into the bonds of marriage, Carol. You must tell me about the hearts that you have broken."

"Not now, Ricardo," she smiled at him benignly. "I'm hot and dusty, and I'm going upstairs to get cleaned up before dinner. Will you tell Juanita that Ian is going to be here?"

"I will indeed," he said, but instead of going off on his errand he watched her go all the way up the staircase and along the gallery past the other bedrooms to her own at the end. He was still standing there when she closed her door behind her.

Dinner that evening was an informal affair with only desultory conversation. Ian was unusually quiet, and Carol had the impression that he and Juanita were waiting for the meal to be over and for her to retire so that they could settle down to a long evening together.

She took the hint as soon as she had finished her coffee. "I think I'll take myself off to bed now," she said. "What time do you want to leave in the morning, Ian?"

"Good and early. Eight o'clock sharp. Better be down here at half-past seven."

The orders were being barked out again. It seemed that that was the only way he knew how to address her. It was on the tip of her tongue to call him "sir" again, but she refrained—Juanita might miss the point and think she meant it seriously, enjoying the servile attitude toward her man.

Ian however seemed to read her thoughts, because he followed up with, "If that isn't too early for you, Carol." Almost politely.

She smiled at him broadly. She was definitely making ground.

In bed she tried to read the paperback she had bought at Kennedy Airport, but she found it hard to concentrate. The events of the day crowded in upon her, the sounds, smells, and sensations—particularly she couldn't forget the extraordinary sensation when Ian had tucked that netting into her collar . . . She put her hand to her throat to try to recapture it, but it had gone. She had never felt anything like it with Edward's most intimate caresses.

Finally she left her bed and opened the glass door onto her balcony. She was about to take off her negligee and turn out the light when a fearful flapping noise filled the room. A huge black shape was careening round and round above her head. At first she thought it was a bird that had flown in from outside attracted by the light, but then it clung to the edge of the canopy over her bed, and hung down, misshapen and ugly. She recognized it then—a bat!

She let out a tiny scream and fled for the door, knocking over a chair on the way. Bolting into the passage she slammed the door behind her and stood there staring at it, panting with fright. What on earth could she do now?

The question was answered for her by Ricardo. He came out of his room next door and inquired in an alarmed voice, "Carol, what's the matter?" His eyes also opened wide when he saw her flimsy nightclothes and her hair streaming over her face. Never mind, she thought, I need his gallantry now.

"There's . . . there's a bat in my room," she gasped. "No, no, I'm perfectly all right, thank you," she added as Ricardo approached with the obvious intention of taking her into his arms for protection. "But, please, could you get the bat out? I'm scared to death of them."

Ricardo cautiously opened the door of her room and peered in. Carol retreated down the passage. She was about opposite the door of his room when the bat flew out over Ricardo's head and started making circles in the passage. Without hesitation she ran into Ricardo's room and shut the door behind her. She stood silent, listening at the keyhole, waiting for developments.

A moment later she heard the sound of her glass balcony door being shut, then his footsteps, before Ricardo pushed open the door of his own room, and she stood back to let him in.

"Did you get rid of it?" she asked.

"Yes, I drove it out of your window and closed it. You're quite safe now."

"Oh, thank you so much. I know it's silly of me but . . ."

"You're shivering, my poor little one. Here, let me comfort . . ." He came toward her again, but she dodged under his outstretched arm and retreated into the passage.

"Thank you again, Ricardo," she whispered, tiptoeing nimbly out of his domain. That was when she saw the shadowy figure of Ian come out of his bedroom and watch her exit from Ricardo's, her furtive steps down the hall, and her surreptitious entrance into her own room. She knew it must have looked bad to him.

At breakfast next morning Carol recounted the incident of the bat. "I don't know what I would have done without Ricardo," she finished.

"You could have called me," Ian said sullenly. He had been looking decidedly sour all through the story.

"I thought you were downstairs," she countered. "And I didn't want to disturb you . . . two nights in a row. Anyway, Ricardo came to my rescue."

"It's amazing how he reacts to a damsel in distress," put in Juanita. "He usually won't go near a bat. You must have made a hit with him, Carol." The idea obviously pleased her.

Ricardo spluttered into his coffee but refrained from comment.

"Hurry up, Carol. We've got to leave right away," said Ian in his exasperated parent's voice, pushing back his chair. He added casually, "Oh, Juanita, I'll be back again this evening if you'll have me."

Juanita's face lit up. "Darling, that's marvelous! I hadn't expected to see you again for days. I tell you what, we'll have a dinner party. I'll ask the Roldans, and we'll all get dressed up."

"That would be fun," Ian agreed. "It's time Carol met a woman like Marilyn, and Ricardo enjoys discussing politics with Pedro."

"Who are the Roldans?" asked Carol.

"Pedro's a Peruvian business friend of Ricardo's, and Marilyn's his English wife," Juanita replied. "You'll really like them." She was being remarkably cordial to Carol this morning.

As soon as they were in the jeep on their way to the boat dock, Ian smacked Carol with the accusation she had been dreading and had tried to avoid by mentioning the bat herself. "You don't expect me to believe that cock-and-bull story you told at breakfast, do you?"

"Why not, Ian?" She tried to sound innocent.

"Because it's a lot of baloney, that's why. I noticed Ricardo didn't back you up."

"He didn't deny it either."

Ian gave a hollow laugh. "You're seen creeping out of a man's room in your nightgown in the middle of the night . . ."

"It was *not* the middle of the night. And anyway, what business is it of yours? I'm here this morning to work for you. What more do you want?"

"I don't want you making a fool of yourself, particularly with that . . . that Ricardo. He has quite a reputation around town, you know. And a pompous idiot into the bargain. You must be pretty desperate for sex to sink that low."

Carol flared up with anger. "You can stop your rotten insinuations right now. I won't have you interfering in my personal life. I'm going to move out of that house tomor-

54

row and get my own apartment in the city—then I can do what I want without you snooping around . . ."

"No, you can't do that. I forbid it!" Ian's voice had risen to an unusual pitch. "I want you where I can keep an eye on you. You're my responsibility here."

"How can you do that when you're up at the camp nearly all the time?"

"From now on I'm not going to be. The work is easing off up there, and I can easily come back in the evenings . . . Besides, its lonely with nobody but old Henry Todd to talk to, and he likes to go to bed early."

So that's it, Carol thought, he can't bear to be parted from his Juanita for more than a few hours at a time now. That necklace must have made her turn on the charm even stronger . . .

They had reached the dock by now, and in the boat Ian didn't seem to want to pursue the matter any further, particularly when the noise of the engine meant that they would have to sit huddled close together to be heard. The journey up river was made in silence. Carol sat there cursing her bad luck last night.

When Henry and Jutai had gathered on the camp jetty to meet them, Ian announced, "The routine's the same as yesterday." At noon he would see sick patients in the medical office, leaving Carol and Henry to continue with the immunization. That way he hoped to have everybody in the nearest village inoculated by the end of the day's work. "I definitely have to leave by five," he stated. "By the way, Jutai, she was delighted with the necklace. It looked so pretty on her."

"I am glad," said Jutai. "It will be something from her homeland she can take with her when she goes away."

Yes, it will be quite a talkpiece in New York City, thought Carol—very fitting for the wife of an expert on tropical diseases.

All morning she injected doses of serum into the arms of the waiting Indians. There was no shyness or reluctance today; those who had been inoculated yesterday must have given a good account of their experience, because they had their arms positioned to receive their shots while they

55

were still well back in the queue. Henry didn't have to do any cajoling.

Soon after Ian and Jutai had disappeared to the office to deal with his patients there, Henry suggested that they break for lunch.

"Don't you think Ian will expect me to keep going?" Carol asked doubtfully. "I don't want to incur his wrath like I did yesterday. I'll be in trouble if I'm not finished by five."

"There must have been something else bothering him to make him blow up at you like he did," Henry reassured her. "He's a strange man, a very conscientious one as far as his work is concerned, but recently he has become moody quite a lot of the time when we're sitting together in the evenings."

"He told me this morning that he intends to come back to Iquitos at night in the future."

"Is that so?" Henry raised his eyebrows. "Well, I can't say I'm sorry. It's been nice to have had his company for the last two months, but an old man enjoys his solitude as well. I find the birds and animals around here all the company I need."

When Henry had explained to the group of Indians still awaiting Carol's attention that they should return in half an hour, they ambled off to stretch themselves out for a midday snooze, and he led her over to what served as a dining table, summoning his cook to bring some food.

Two plates of risotto made with pork arrived almost at once—wild boar Henry said it was, and quite delicious—and they washed it down with glasses of passion fruit juice. Carol commented favorably on the meal.

"I manage to eat well without bringing anything except powdered milk in from outside," he said with pride, and added with a twinkle, "We even distill our own rum from some sugar cane I planted. After a couple of my drinks, even Ian becomes quite chatty."

"What does he talk about?" she asked. "Since I met him in Iquitos, he hasn't mentioned anything except our job here."

"Oh, he tells me about his schooling in Europe sometimes—his father sent him for training in Madrid and Paris, you know—that's where he learnt Spanish, as well as developing his interest in opera."

"Yes, I'd heard about that," Carol smiled at the recollection of the first time she had set eyes on him. "I believe he has quite a good voice himself."

"Does he? He plays his tapes sometimes on the machine I use to record bird calls—personally I prefer the bird calls."

Carol grinned sympathetically. "Well, you won't have to put up with his music anymore, Henry."

"So you say. Why is he moving back to Iquitos? To be near Juanita Muñoz?"

"I'm sure that's the reason. But he also seems intent on not letting me out of his sight . . ."

"Now that I can understand . . ."

"No, no, Henry, it's not that at all. He regards me as a responsibility—like a naughty child—someone who might spoil his good name for him because we work together. It's all come about because of a ridiculous incident last night."

And so she came to tell Henry about Ricardo and the bat, and Ian's suspicion of her.

Henry was aghast. "How could he think that of you, Carol! It's absurd. I'll talk to him before you leave this afternoon."

"Well, if you think it would do any good . . ." Carol said dubiously. "He certainly won't listen to me."

Henry's opportunity came later in the day while Carol was busy at her inoculations. Ian came out of the medical office and started walking, head down, preoccupied, across the camp. Henry left her side and stomped over to catch up with him. She saw Ian look surprised, and then a little annoyed, as the old man lectured him. He stole a glance in her direction at one point; she felt herself blushing and turned away.

Finally Ian shrugged and walked off. Henry returned to say that Ian didn't seem entirely convinced that Carol wasn't lying, but that he'd give her the benefit of the doubt provided she'd stay away from Ricardo in future.

"How can I do that? I'm living in his house. And he's

57

kind and attentive, although he doesn't interest me a bit . . ."

At four thirty Carol had no more patients left. She went to the office to put the remainder of the serum back in the refrigerator and to sterilize the equipment ready for the next day. She had her back to the door when she heard a slight sound behind her. She turned round quickly, and there was Ian, so close that she bumped him with her elbow, looking down into her upturned face, familiar crinkles of amusement around his eyes.

"I've got something for you," he said softly. "As a peace offering."

"Oh . . . ?" She found herself tongue-tied, taken by surprise, and gripped by a curious feeling of pleasurable expectation. He was holding one hand behind his back, and with the other he took her hand and drew her nearer. Momentarily she closed her eyes as her head began to swim . . .

"Don't you want to see what I've got?" he teased her.

"Yes . . . yes, what have you got?" The words stumbled out as she brought his handsome face into focus again.

He whipped the other hand from behind his back and presented her with . . . an orchid. Its petals were the most delicate she had ever seen, a very deep purple, nearly black. She took it from him, holding it as though it might break.

"Did . . . did you climb a tree for it?" she asked.

He nodded. "I wanted a blue one—they're the rarest of all, but I couldn't find one in time. I wanted to give it to you this afternoon." As he said it he squeezed her fingers gently, emphasizing his need to make up after their quarrel.

"I see. You believe me now—is that it?"

"It doesn't matter whether I do or not." He let her hand go, and her heartbeat began to return to normal. "I'm

"That's nice of you. I'd rather you believed me."
prepared to forget the whole thing on two conditions."

"I would, Carol, if I didn't know Ricardo. I'm sure he somehow inveigled you into his room last night, so I don't blame you. Which brings me to my first condition. That you stay away from him as much as you reasonably can."

"What's the other condition?"

58

"That you don't move out of the house."

Carol paused a moment to consider what those conditions implied. Ricardo would be no problem—she would have kept him at bay anyhow until he finally gave up chasing her. But to agree to stay in the Muñoz villa meant surrendering some of her own liberty. She would remain under Ian's watchful and suspicious eye day and night. To offset that were the financial benefits and another, less tangible, advantage. Incomprehensible though it might be, she had to admit that she wanted to stay near to Ian Morrison.

"You mean I'm to exchange my personal freedom for an orchid?" she asked with an impish grin.

"Not your freedom. Call it an interest in your activities. And something else comes with the orchid—our friendship."

"All right, master," she said. "I give up. I am yours to command."

"Good," he said, straightening his back as though he had just concluded a successful deal. "Then let's go back and enjoy Juanita's dinner party tonight."

In her room that evening she spent a long time on her hair, her make-up, and her clothes. She parted her hair so that it hung loose over one eye and was swept in a shining auburn roll behind her ear on the other side. It was a style that she hadn't worn for some time—Edward had said it made her look too seductive. She applied liberal amounts of eye-shadow and mascara and softened her generous mouth with lip-gloss. Her appearance in the mirror pleased her—she had spent too much time lately as the efficient nurse. Tonight for some reason she felt deliciously feminine.

Her choice of clothes was limited by the amount she had been able to bring with her in a suitcase. She was very tempted to wear the long, dark blue silk dress that she had persuaded Edward to buy for her at a new French boutique in Albany but which he subsequently disapproved of, because of its daring halter top. From the back it looked as though she had nothing on above the waist. Reluctantly she hung it up again in her closet and selected a dark green skirt and a simple cream-colored blouse of spotless crêpe de Chine. With black open-toed sandals she looked properly demure—the blue silk might have incited Ricardo to a degree of amorousness that she would have difficulty controlling—but she added a touch of whimsy to her ensemble by tying a little green velvet ribbon around her throat. At the last minute she picked up the black orchid, which Ian had given her, and pinned it to the copper belt around her waist. Its lustrous sheen stood out vividly against her blouse.

Finally satisfied, she made her way downstairs to the large, sumptuous sitting room from which she could already hear sounds of conversation and laughter.

Ricardo jumped up from a deep chair with as much agility as his corpulence would allow. "Carol, if you will allow me to say so, you look exquisite."

She acknowledged his compliment with a brief, tolerant smile before her attention was arrested by the transformation in Ian's appearance. He had also risen and was standing comfortably by his chair gazing at her with undisguised approval. He looked as though he never dressed in anything but immaculate tailoring in his life. The jacket of his white flannel suit hung easily from his broad shoulders, and the perfectly cut pants that fell from his belt to a pair of white buckskin shoes added to his already impressive height. A dark blue shirt and tie completed the picture of suave elegance.

She tore her eyes away from the stunning vision Ian presented to concentrate on the introductions Juanita was making. The short, tubby man whose heavy black sideburns emphasized his completely bald head was Pedro Roldan, and the jolly blonde in her late thirties was his wife, Marilyn. Marilyn looked like a buxom English barmaid in her creased print. The Roldans greeted Carol affably, and she took her place on the sofa beside Marilyn.

"What kind of a drink can I fetch for you?" Ricardo was asking her. "Would you like one of my rum concoctions?"

"We call them the Cuzco Specials," Marilyn nudged her. "After the town fifteen thousand feet high in Central Peru.

That's the effect they have on you the way Ricardo makes them."

"Thank you, Ricardo," said Carol. "But keep mine down to five thousand feet, would you. My boss is watching me."

She glanced across at Ian, who was smiling benignly. "Remind me to let you try some manioc some time," he said. "That's the drink the Yaguas make from fermented cassava flour, using the yeast from their own mouths to ferment it."

"That doesn't sound at all sanitary for a public health nurse to drink," was her enjoinder. "I think I'd prefer Henry Todd's homemade rum."

"What!" exclaimed Ian in mock horror. "Has old Henry been plying you with strong drink while my back was turned?"

"No, but he's been telling me how you become quite chatty after one or two."

"I must keep you away from Henry in the future," he went on in the same tone. "He'll be letting out state secrets next."

Juanita interrupted their lighthearted banter with a loud remark to Pedro Roldan about the recent experiment to import and raise cattle on the foothills of the Andes. Carol observed Juanita while she talked. She was looking every inch the temptress tonight. Her clinging purple dress was cut so low at the neck that her breasts swelled up above it, a pendant on a silver chain nestling in the cleavage.

The discussion on cattle raising died quickly. Marilyn broke the awkward lull that followed. "Carol, how did you find that lovely orchid? Those gorgeous black ones only grow about twenty feet off the ground."

"Ian got it for me," she said. "He can reach up nearly twenty feet. He's a good orchid-giver." She smiled innocently in Ian's direction.

But Ian didn't seem to hear—he was busily retying his shoelace. Juanita heard all right; she was giving Ian such a malevolent stare that, had he been in a position to accept it, he might well have been turned to stone.

At dinner Carol was seated on Ricardo's right—Ricardo

was presiding at the head of the table—and with Pedro Roldan on the other side. Opposite her was Marilyn. Ian sat obliquely across from her, next to Juanita, who, as soon as they had sat down, attacked him with an animated, though whispered, monologue, which he didn't seem to be much enjoying. Carol felt sure Juanita was berating Ian for picking her the orchid; surely it was only good manners to wear a gift that one has just received when the giver is present at the same dinner party. She wondered why Juanita wasn't wearing the necklace she had been given yesterday—it was a far more valuable present than a single orchid blossom.

The first course was *ceviche*, a cold fish soup, which Ricardo told her was a Mexican specialty adopted in one form or another by all the South American countries. He and Pedro were spooning their portions in with great zest, and Marilyn appeared to like it too, but Carol could barely swallow half her bowlful. Guiltily she caught Ian's eye—wrinkling up her nose in distaste with a meaningful glance at the bowl in front of her. He spluttered into laughter, spilling a spoonful onto the tablecloth, an accident which evoked another withering look from Juanita. Carol decided that she had caused enough friction between Ian and his hostess for one evening. She would have to be more careful from now on.

Halfway through the *carne a la parrilla*, grilled beef with tomatoes and onions, which Carol ate with relish, she became aware that Marilyn was asking her how she liked her job at the camp.

"Very much, thank you," she replied. "It's the most fascinating place I've ever worked in."

"And a fascinating man to work for, too," suggested Marilyn behind her hand, and with a broad wink.

"Oh, I don't know," Carol answered casually. "All doctors are much the same—never give nurses the credit that's due them."

Marilyn made her comment on Ian while Ricardo was walking around the table, playing the genial host with a bottle of wine, but now he returned to his seat and started a conversation with Carol. Marilyn had managed to pry

Ian's attention away from Juanita and was holding forth volubly.

"After dinner I must show you my collection of antique guns," said Ricardo with eager enthusiasm. "Many of them date from my great-grandfather's time. The rebellious Indians were no match for the Spanish settlers in those days. The only time the Indians ever won a battle was through treachery."

The topic didn't appeal to Carol at all, considering that she was devoting most of her energies to saving Indians' lives, not massacring them. "I don't really like guns," she said, and then to soften the bluntness of her remark, "Now if you had a collection of butterflies, I'd love to see those. I've spotted some beautiful big ones up at the camp."

"But I have a butterfly collection, too!" Ricardo informed her to her chagrin. "My father put it together. We'll go and look at it as soon as we've had our coffee."

"Oh, I don't know that we should leave the other guests," Carol came back quickly. "Some other time you can show them to me."

Ricardo was not to be put off so easily, insisting that the Roldans were old friends who didn't need him to entertain them every minute they were in his house. As soon as everybody got up from the table, he led her firmly out of the room. Carol couldn't have broken loose from his unwelcome grip on her arm without creating a scene. She hoped at least that Ian would see that she was being forcibly abducted, but unfortunately he had his back to her at that moment.

The butterflies were housed in some dusty glass cases in a little-used room at the other end of the house. Their dead wings had none of the frivolous delicacy of living butterflies. Ricardo strained to read the faded labels attached to each one and finally gave up feigning interest for the sake of appearances.

"Carol," he said gravely, turning away from the cases to face her, "I just want you to know that if that scoundrel Morrison's treatment of you becomes intolerable, you have only to tell me and I will gladly give you all the support

63

you need. I think it's disgraceful the way he talks to you."

"I'm quite capable of looking after myself, thank you, Ricardo," she answered in a firm, steady voice, her arms folded across her chest to forestall any physically protective instincts he might have. "Ian knows how I feel about his rather, er, straightforward way of handing out criticism, and I'm sure that as we get to know each other better, he will change his attitude."

"Carol, you're not being fair to yourself. He's a brute, a callous brute, and I'm not one to sit and watch him brutalize a sweet, gentle girl . . ." Ricardo took a pace forward, his eyes gleaming with outrage, intent on enfolding her in his brawny arms in spite of her firm stance.

Carol tensed. "I'm not so sweet and gentle as you think." Ricardo let his arms drop to his sides, so Carol decided to use their moment of privacy to ask him something that had been worrying her. "Tell me, if you dislike Ian so much, why do you seem so pleased about him becoming your brother-in-law?"

He shrugged his shoulders in the Latin manner. "What does it matter to me what kind of man he is? Juanita is in love with him and wants to marry him—that's all that counts. If they get married, he will take her off to New York, and I will be rid of them both."

Carol raised her eyebrows. "You want to get rid of your sister? I thought . . ."

"Oh, I'm very fond of Juanita as my little sister. But now she is older, she has developed expensive-tastes, more than even I can afford. And I'm a rich man, Carol; make no mistake about that. But there are limits, and I have other ideas about how to spend my wealth. A wife of my own, for example . . ."

Carol cut into Ricardo's explanation. She had her answer, and there was something else he had said which intrigued her. "So it isn't definite yet that Ian is going to marry Juanita? I thought you said that they were engaged, although I've noticed that she isn't wearing a ring."

"They are as good as betrothed, it is true. But Juanita is a Catholic, and Ian is not, and there is some delay on that account. It would be better if you didn't make any public reference to their forthcoming marriage. Discretion is important at this stage. But I'm glad to say I have no doubt about the eventual outcome."

"I see," said Carol quietly.

"Now, my dearest Carol, let me show you the rest of the house." He stepped forward again and took hold of her shoulders. She didn't move, lost in thought, hardly aware of his presence. "As I told you, I have great plans for renovating . . ."

Carol still didn't blink an eyelid. She was visualizing an imaginary scene, a church with an organ playing, Juanita in a long white veil with a tall man standing beside her. . . .

"Carol, you're not listening. Perhaps this will wake you up." Before she knew what was happening, Ricardo had planted his mouth on hers in a damp, uninspiring kiss. He held it there for a second.

"Your guests are missing you, Ricardo." Ian's frigid voice was speaking from the open doorway.

When the three of them filed back into the living room, Juanita was putting some music on the record player. Pedro was helping her make a choice, and neither of them noticed the trio enter. But Marilyn looked up from her seat on the sofa, agog with interest, and beckoned to Carol to come and sit beside her.

"What was going on?" she asked, her big blue eyes popping out of her head at the thought of some juicy gossip. "I saw Ricardo lead you out after dinner, but didn't think anything of it until Ian asked me if I knew where you were. He looked absolutely livid when I told him."

"Exactly what did you say, Marilyn?"

"Well, I said I saw you go out together, and that you didn't look too anxious to go. I'd noticed your beseeching glance in Ian's direction."

"Did you tell Ian about that?"

"Yes, I did. I hope I didn't do anything wrong."

Carol felt like hugging the bouncy little woman. "You certainly didn't. You may have saved my life. Ian doesn't like my having anything to do with Ricardo."

"Why not? Is he jealous? Does he want you for himself

then? How exciting for you to be fought over by two gorgeous men!"

"Ian's just afraid that if I get involved in any kind of
private life, my job at the camp will suffer."

"And what about Ricardo? He seemed awfully keen to
take you outside." Marilyn was obviously after all the
gruesome details, and Carol didn't want to snub her. After
all, her nosiness had paid off in that she had told Ian
about her reluctance to go with Ricardo.

"Oh, you know these South Americans," said Carol before she realized what a brick she was dropping.

Marilyn laughed. "I do indeed. I'm married to one. But
Ricardo isn't like that—or hasn't been for some time. His
fiancée died last year, you know. The poor boy was terribly upset. You're the first girl he's looked at for ages."

Carol's eyes opened wide in surprise. "Is that so? I understood he had quite a reputation as a lady's man."

"Far from it. Who told you that?"

"Well, Ian did, as a matter of fact. He doesn't seem to
like Ricardo very much."

"I can't understand that," said Marilyn with a puzzled
frown. "They used to be such good friends. That's why he
invited Ian to come and stay in this house when he wanted
to get away from the camp. Something must have come
between them. I must ask Pedro—he'll know."

Carol felt it was time to change the subject. Any problems between the two men were no business of hers. But
whatever they were, she hoped they would soon be
resolved. It made the atmosphere uncomfortable in the
house, and if they became friends again, Ian might be
more tolerant about relations between her and Ricardo.
Although he didn't excite her, she was rather flattered to
think that she was the first girl he had taken an interest in
since the unfortunate death of his fiancée.

"What do you do with your time, Marilyn?" asked
Carol. "I imagine you have servants to look after your
house like everyone else here. Or does your English background make you want to do it all yourself?"

"Oh no, I'm a hopeless housekeeper. I fill in time by
working as a typist. Not many people can type in English

in this town. Actually I type out Ian's letters and reports for him. I remember when he wrote to the States advertising for a nurse to come out here and help him."

"Did he specify what kind of person he wanted?"

"No, he said he thought he'd be lucky to get anyone. He must be very pleased to have you. Why did you come here, Carol?"

Carol was glad she didn't have to go into the painful story of Edward again, because some soft music had replaced the heavy rumba beat that had been successfully drowning her conversation with Marilyn from anyone else's ears, and Ricardo was standing before them, requesting Marilyn to dance. Carol noticed that he studiously ignored her own presence.

Marilyn accepted graciously with a word to Carol that they must get together and gossip some more some time, and Carol settled back into the cushions, lighting one of her rare cigarettes. Pedro took Juanita to dance. It amused Carol to watch them, because in her heels Juanita was taller than he was, and one of the enormous gold loops that she was wearing as earrings kept getting hooked round Pedro's nose or into his mouth, disturbing the close clinch in which he held her. Juanita was unaware of this and danced with passionate sensuousness, even with Pedro. Carol gulped at the thought of how she must arouse Ian when she set her mind to it.

Ian was now the only man not dancing, and inevitably he came over to take her to the floor. He has to, thought Carol, it would look funny if he didn't, but how he must hate doing it! She smiled at him when he asked her, and stubbed out her cigarette.

"You shouldn't smoke those things," he said tersely. "They're bad for you."

"I only do when I'm waiting for something dreadful to happen. Well, let's get it over with—what's my punishment?"

He stood without moving when she put her hand on his shoulder, ready to start dancing. "I'm sorry I didn't see your signal for help," he said in a gentler tone. "Marilyn told me about it afterward, so I can't blame you for going with Ricardo. But you needn't have let him kiss you like that."

"It wasn't like anything if you want to know."

"I noticed you weren't putting up any resistance."

"I was hardly aware it was going on. I . . . was thinking about something else."

"Oh, don't be absurd, Carol! You didn't even know when a man was kissing you? What was it you were thinking about?"

"Another man, as a matter of fact."

"Oh, your ex-fiancé, eh? The one who's too damn much like me. Well, let's see if you can keep on thinking about him while *I* try to distract you. Here goes!"

He slipped both hands round her waist and drew her to him, at the same time softly brushing her lips with his. Unconsciously the hand she had on his shoulder slipped around his neck, and they stood there clasped in each other's arms for a long second. Carol felt the ground fall away beneath her. All she could hear was the wild beating of her heart as his firm, cool lips explored hers.

Almost at once his hips started swaying in time to the music, and she moved with him. His hand grasped hers as his cheek slipped over tenderly to rest against her own. They were dancing now, him turning her toward the other two couples, neither of whom could have noticed the kiss.

"Ian," she whispered, "what if Juanita had seen?"

"Oh, she's used to her guests kissing each other. Her brother does it all the time."

His flippant tone surprised her. How refreshing it is to hear him talk with such cheerful abandon, she thought. He's almost beginning to think of me as a woman after all, and not just as his faithful helper.

He held her away to gaze into her eyes. "Well, is your mind still far off in distant Albany with your ex-boyfriend?"

She shook her head, smiling with sheer contentment, and pressed her cheek once more to his. But after a few more steps he held her back again and said, more seriously this time, "You shouldn't have worn that orchid, you know. Juanita was upset."

The hand of his that she was holding suddenly felt cold. Carol reminded herself sternly that Ian was someone else's man, one whom she had borrowed for a fleeting instant, and must now return. "I'm sorry," she said. "I didn't think. Was she very annoyed?"

"She's trying to encourage a relationship between you and Ricardo—not that it needs much encouraging from what I've seen—and she's afraid that you wearing my orchid might put him off."

Don't kid me that that was why she was upset, Carol thought. She was jealous, that's all. If only she knew how little she had to be jealous about; even Ian's kiss had been no more than a petty joke to him.

"I don't like Juanita to get miffed at me," Ian was saying. "I need her too much. Especially since Ricardo turned against me . . ."

"What have you got against Ricardo, Ian?" Carol asked. "The blatant animosity between you two doesn't make for a happy atmosphere in the house. He's really quite sweet, you know."

Ian's features froze into the hard, grim countenance Carol had had to endure so much of lately. "I don't enjoy hearing you say that sort of thing about him, Carol. You don't know the man as well as I do. And if you again let yourself get lured into a dark corner with him, I'll know you did it on purpose, and I'll be . . . be very disappointed in you."

"That'll be a change. I only wish you were as appreciative of me as he is." They had stopped dancing now. Her hand had come off his shoulder, and they were standing apart, confronting each other.

"He's in no position to judge you, as he doesn't work with you, whereas I do. My only concerns are to keep you efficient and keep you out of trouble, and I can't do either without criticizing you, so you better get used to it. By the way, I want all the people in the other village inoculated by tomorrow, so don't be late in the morning."

Carol went off to her room as soon as the Roldans had said good night. Ian's rough words had deflated her once more, and she had had to force herself to smile at Marilyn's giggling caution against forceful South Americans. "Keep in touch, lovie," Marilyn had said. "I want to hear the sequel to that exciting episode." Ricardo and Juanita saw the Roldans out, leaving Ian and Carol alone in the sitting room for a moment before she left.

"I'm going to bed now," she said flatly. "I'll see you in the morning. And don't worry, I won't be late."

"Good night, Carol," he replied. "And thank you for the dance. I enjoyed it."

Sighing, she turned her back on him and went upstairs, flopping onto her bed for a few minutes' peace before she got undressed. Her mind was in a turmoil. Two men had kissed her that night, one as a sort of protective gesture against the other, and the second to take her mind off a third, Edward. As if her mind had ever been on the third—he had only assumed it was. She had hardly ever thought about Edward in the last few days. If only Ian would realize that—if only he would realize that Ricardo didn't mean anything to her either—if only he didn't disturb her so much . . .

Closing her eyes she pictured him in his white suit, handsome, debonair, fully in charge of any situation that might present itself. She felt again the pressure of his cool lips on hers. Not since she was a gawky teen-ager had she reacted with such emotion to a kiss. How had she come to allow this strong-willed, demanding man to interfere so much with her normally rational approach to life?

Several hours later she had recovered her composure and drifted off to sleep, firmly resolved that Ian Morrison would have no further influence on her personality or her emotions.

Chapter 4

The trip up river next morning started as before. Antonio drove the boat at his usual breakneck speed, cutting across the wake of a larger vessel at one point without slowing down and causing the boat to lurch dangerously. The jolt threw Carol sideways off her seat; she would have pitched onto the deck if Ian hadn't reached out to hold her upright.

She expected some caustic remark about her not being much of a sailor, but he just laughed and yelled against the noise, "Steady there! We don't want to lose you before we even arrive."

His mood was cheerful this morning. He must have slept longer than she had—either that or Juanita had entertained him satisfactorily after the party had broken up last night. The memory of their embraces probably accounted for the self-satisfied grin on his face. Carol suddenly felt unaccountably angry with Juanita for bringing Ian happiness, even though she herself was now benefitting from his mood.

The boat turned into the creek, and Carol grimaced at the innocent-looking reeds she had so foolishly cut her hand on the first time they had come up here. She hoped that she had now committed the last of the stupid blunders that annoyed Ian so much. Full of optimism and looking forward to her day's work, she raised her eyes to the camp jetty, which they were now rapidly approaching.

Jutai was on the jetty with another Indian, a squat, heavily-built man wearing nothing but a loincloth. Jutai was waving both arms in excitement. He seemed to be in a hurry for them to arrive, as though he had some news of great importance to impart. Carol wondered what it could be—how could anything of unusual significance happen in this isolated camp or in the villages surrounding it, where life proceeded every day exactly as it had for hundreds of years?

Ian had noticed Jutai's gesticulations too. "It looks as though he has something to tell us, Carol. Be prepared for the worst. If anything different happens in this place, it's always bad."

Ian was first up the ladder with Carol hard on his heels. "Well, Jutai," he said, "What is it? What's the disaster this time?"

"Doctor," said Jutai, his face grave as he indicated the man beside him, "this is my cousin Mono from the village of Pucallpa, twenty miles inland through the jungle. He has paddled his canoe all night to come here."

"Why? What's the problem at Pucallpa?" Ian asked.

"The white man's disease," said Jutai with awe. "It has claimed many victims in the village. Babies very ill. Two old men already dead."

Ian turned to Carol. "The white man's disease is measles. Someone from the village down here must have carried it up to Pucallpa. That's too bad. I had hoped that it wouldn't spread."

"What do we do now?" asked Carol.

"We leave right away to go up there. Me to treat the sick, and you to inoculate the rest of the village as quickly as you can. Pucallpa's the place where I'm studying the babies and. . . ."

"How do we get there?"

"The way this man came down. By canoe. There's no road. Jutai, tell your cousin to get back to Pucallpa right away—he can paddle his one-man canoe a lot faster than we can—and tell the head man that I'm on my way. Only white doctor can stop the white man's disease—make sure he understands that and stops the local witch doctor from burning the patient's skin or trying any of his other so-called treatments."

Jutai babbled away in his own language at Mono. Mono

argued a bit at first, but Jutai asserted his authority, and the other reluctantly accepted it.

"And tell him to put all the sick people in one house and not let anyone else in except the mothers to feed their babies. The nurse and I will be there this evening. Come on, Carol, this is where your real work begins."

"You mean I get to wear my jungle outfit at last?"

"You'll certainly need it on this trip. Every time I go to Pucallpa, I wonder if I'll ever make it back again. The going gets tougher as the creek gets narrower."

"How long do you think we will be away?" The prospect of disappearing into the wilds with Ian appealed to her enormously.

"About four days altogether, I should think. I'll send Antonio down to Iquitos with a message, so they won't worry." Ian didn't seem in the least distressed about being away from the Muñozes. He was acting as excited over their imminent adventure as she was. Carol found this strange, considering how adamant he had been a couple of days ago to return to the villa every night. She would have thought that Juanita would have whetted his ardor even more since then.

"Okay, I'll go and get changed," she said. "And I'll pack up the syringes and other equipment and fill the serum container with fresh ice from the refrigerator."

"That's my girl! Your brain's really ticking today." He smiled at her, and she was overjoyed to see those crinkles appear round his eyes as he did.

"What about food? Can I do anything about that too?"

"No, don't worry about that. I'll get Jutai to bring along what we'll need. We'll take him with us because I couldn't trust myself to find the way. And he'll be a useful hand with a paddle. You don't mind paddling, do you, Carol?"

What's come over the man? she thought. He's never asked me if I *minded* doing anything before. "Of course not!" she replied. "I used to be pretty hot stuff on the lake in Albany Park."

"Albany Park, New York . . ." he mused. "That seems a long way away right now, doesn't it?" He turned away with an abrupt, "See you soon then."

Carol went off to collect the immunization materials with a step as light as if she was on air. What a trip this was going to be, and what a marvelous companion to be going with!

Jutai was waiting in the canoe when she emerged from the empty hut she had used as a changing room. The safari suit felt comfortably snug around her hips and bust, and the lightweight topee on her head with its veil of mosquito netting felt natural and appropriate on her head. She loaded her packages into the canoe and sat down on the edge of the dock, happily swinging her legs.

Jutai smiled up at her, showing several gold front teeth. "You like to go into the jungle, nurse-lady?" he asked.

"I can't wait," she smiled back. "It's not frightening, is it, Jutai?"

"No . . . but necessary to be careful," he warned. "Piranhas, crocodiles, poison snakes. Never to go walk in jungle alone—always take Jutai. Jutai know to keep lady out of danger."

"I'll feel very safe with you along," she said. "Do you ever take your daughter, Chicua, into the jungle?"

Jutai beamed with pride at his daughter's name. "Chicua know more about jungle than her father. Chicua know more about everything than her father—and she only eleven years old!"

"I hear she's going to be a doctor one day."

Jutai's expression clouded slightly. "You tell me, señorita, is okay for girl to be doctor? Many girls nurses, yes, but doctor . . . that is man's job, no?"

"Oh, no, Jutai. Lots of girls become doctors these days. I know some very good ones. And by the time Chicua graduates, lady doctors will be accepted by the Indians, too. All the young girls will look up to her and want to be doctors too, you'll see."

"I wish I able to help her in school," he said wistfully. "But me, I only know native doctor medicine, mumbo jumbo you call it."

"I don't call it mumbo jumbo," Carol said indignantly. "I'm sure your knowledge of plants and herbs has helped many people."

74

"Señor Todd understand too, and he very wise man. Only Señor Morrison not believe any good."

"That's because Señor Morrison has only been here a few months and has been so busy practicing his kind of medicine that he hasn't had time to study yours. Perhaps Chicua will explain it to him one day."

Jutai nodded enthusiastically. "I hope that. Señor Morrison very good to Chicua—pay for her in school. He call Chicua his . . ."

"Come on, Jutai, not so much talk." Ian's voice came from behind where Carol was sitting on the dock, which also hid his approach from Jutai in the canoe below. "Let's be on our way. All set, Carol?"

"Never more so," she answered, slithering down into the middle seat in the canoe. Jutai was occupying the front one, and Ian was already climbing into the one behind.

Jutai pushed off from the pilings, and they floated silently out into the stream, picking up their paddles for the start of an adventure such as Carol would have considered unthinkable only a few weeks earlier. She would also have considered it unthinkable a few weeks ago that she would be drawing such strength and confidence from a new man, the man who now sat behind her and with whom she looked forward to sharing so much, not only on this trip, but for as long as he wanted her to work for him.

They were traveling as light as possible, in case it was necessary to portage the canoe across dry land at some point. Jutai had stacked the immunization equipment up in the bow, and Ian had put his medical bag and two small pup tents under his seat. Cans of corned beef, vegetables, and fresh water lay beside Carol, along with Ian's expensive camera. Jutai apparently scorned protective clothing, but Ian had changed into a khaki shirt with an abundance of pockets, pants that tucked into heavy boots, and a mosquito-proof topee just like Carol's. Being similarly dressed added to her sense of comradeship with him.

She dug her paddle into the dark, murky water with firm strokes, taking her timing from Jutai. Behind her, Ian was paddling steadily as well as using his oar as a rudder; she felt the canoe surge forward each time he forced the water back. Their progress up the creek was rapid for the first hour or two, and the twenty miles had shortened to about twelve when Ian called a halt for lunch.

"You're doing well, Carol," he said. "Getting tired?"

In fact, her muscles were aching badly, but there was no way she would admit to weakness as long as she could still make another stroke. "Not really, but I'm ready for a little rest," she said, twisting her neck to smile at him. He gave her an encouraging pat on the shoulder, and she felt new strength seep into her body from his hand.

Their difficulties began in the early afternoon. The creek narrowed until, in places, it closed in on them so much that the creeping liana hanging down from giant trees on either side brushed against their faces. Jutai often had to lift low, overhanging branches so that Carol could duck under them and then pass them back to Ian, a slow process, which hindered them greatly. Sometimes the bottom of the canoe stuck on a submerged log, and Jutai had to ease it across with his paddle. The sunlight became completely blocked out by the dense forest meeting overhead; the air above the strip of water grew dank and heavy. Raucous calls from brightly colored parrots rent the silence, unseen animals rustled the undergrowth, and mosquitoes pinged insistently outside Carol's netting.

She would have become frightened had it not been for Ian's unflagging good spirits. "This is just a bad spot," he would say. "It soon gets easier," or, "More exciting than Albany Park, eh, Carol?" She couldn't disagree with him on that.

But they were still some miles from their destination when darkness began to fall. The jungle came alive with a cacophony of screeching birds; yelping monkeys bounced through the branches; and on one occasion Jutai gestured for silence, pointing to a mud bank where the long, dark shape of a crocodile could be seen slithering noiselessly into the water only a few feet ahead.

It was soon after that when Ian announced, "Okay, this is it. We can't make it to Pucallpa tonight. We'll camp here and go on tomorrow."

They were opposite a pleasant grassy clearing onto

which the last rays of sun still shone. A fallen tree trunk provided a convenient landing place with fairly deep water; by walking along it they would be able to reach dry land without wading through mud. An overhanging branch would make disembarkation easier.

Jutai heaved the serum and other equipment ashore and stepped out to secure the boat. Ian lifted out his medical bag and the rolled-up tents before climbing out too. Then Carol stood up to follow them onto the tree trunk, but after so long in a crouched position, a sudden dizziness came over her—she clutched for the overhanging branch and to regain her balance trod heavily on the side of the canoe . . .

A split second later she was left dangling from the branch, and the canoe was capsized beneath her.

Ian's strong arms pulled her to safety. She stood there on the trunk holding onto him until the shaking of her body had subsided and had been replaced by a warm sense of peace, as if she had awakened from a nightmare and found herself in bed, cozy in his arms. The illusion was strangely real . . . until he held her off from him and fixed her with cold eyes from under a bushy frown.

"What *am I* going to do about you?" he sighed. "Won't you ever learn? Don't you know that you should never stand on the edge of a canoe?"

"I . . . I'm sorry," she blurted, humiliated and miserable. "I felt giddy when I stood up and . . ."

"You shouldn't have stood up in the first place. However, there's no harm done, fortunately. We can easily right the canoe. . . . Hey, wait a minute, where's my camera? It was still in the boat." Ian released Carol abruptly and went onto his knees, reaching for the canoe's hull.

Helplessly she watched as the two men turned the boat right side up and emptied the water out of it. The camera had vanished into the murky depths below, far too deep for retrieval. And so had all the food.

"I'm terribly sorry, Ian," she moaned. "I'll get you a new camera."

"I can get myself a new camera, thank you. But now suppose you just tell me what we're going to eat."

"I'll find something. There must be something around here, a rabbit or a fish or. . . ."

"There are no rabbits in this country. And the fish don't come this far up the creek." The hard line of his mouth and the icy stare that she had come to dread were back with a vengeance. "And there are no corner grocery stores here either."

His sarcasm cut into her like a knife. New vitality of body and clarity of mind took over as she felt her blood rising. "I said I'll find something, and I will. Now you get a fire going and put up the tents, and I'll come back with dinner in an hour or so," she shot back at him, eyes blazing.

"Well, look who's running the show now," he said with a hollow laugh. But his expression showed more than a hint of admiration.

Carol turned her back on him. "Come on, Jutai. You'll help me, won't you?" Adjusting her hat to a businesslike angle, she stuck her chin in the air and started striding out across the clearing. She knew she had to succeed in her quest if she was ever to regain his respect. She felt as though her whole future depended on her ability to make amends for the stupid error in the boat. But how could she possibly find food for a meal? She knew nothing of jungle life . . .

Jutai caught up with her at the edge of the clearing. "Nurse, I tell you. You not go in there without Jutai. But señorita is quite right. No man ever starve in jungle . . . if he know what to do."

The Indian pulled a knife out of bis belt and cut a length of dead bamboo, squinting down in it to see that it was hollow. Then he found a couple of short pieces of stick that fitted tightly into one end. Satisfied with that, he started searching through the undergrowth until he found some uninteresting-looking red berries. Protecting his fingers with a leaf, he picked several and ground them up on a piece of bark. Next he sharpened one end of each of the sticks until it came to a fine point and dipped the points into the ground-up berries. Finally he inserted one of the sticks into the bamboo with the point sticking out. The whole procedure had only taken five minutes.

"Now we are ready to go hunting," said Jutai. "What would you like to present to Señor Morrison for dinner? a monkey, a possum, or perhaps a hoatzin?"

"What's a hoatzin?" Carol asked doubtfully. "I don't think a monkey or a possum . . ."

"A hoatzin is a native bird to the Amazon. Is like what you call a pheasant, but more large."

"That sounds perfect!" she said. "But how are we going to catch one?"

"You will see," answered Jutai, showing his gold teeth in a broad grin. "I hope we can find one. They are rare, but the sunset is the best time."

Carol followed the little Indian along a rough trail that led out of the clearing. Once he gripped her arm and pulled her to one side as a snake crossed their path. She stifled a scream with her hand and didn't breathe again until it had passed.

Soon Jutai pointed to a fat brown bird sitting in a tree. With a cunning smile he lifted the bamboo blowpipe to his mouth and ballooned his cheeks while taking aim. The arrow popped out of the end and sailed through the air, but missed the bird, which flapped clumsily to another branch. Jutai stalked it closer this time and blew out the second arrow. The hoatzin tried to fly, but quickly fell heavily to the ground as if stunned.

Carol was amazed. "You mean you killed it with a little piece of stick?"

"Berry juice contained curare," he explained, salvaging the bird from the bushes and wringing its neck. "Paralyzes muscles so no more fly. Doctors use curare, too. Señor Morrison interested curare."

"That's marvelous!" said Carol. "Pheasant for dinner tonight. I wonder what we can use for vegetables."

Jutai scoured the ground until he found some three-toed footprints. He followed them into the undergrowth with Carol close behind. They led to a patch of leaves under which Jutai dug with his knife until he came to the roots. They looked like sweet potatoes.

"Yams," he announced with pride. "Wild boar eat them always. Follow prints, find yams."

On the way back to the clearing, Carol spotted some wild asparagus, and they also picked some bananas and juicy ripe papaws for dessert. A hollow tree trunk was full of fresh rainwater. They now had everything they needed for an excellent meal.

As they neared the spot where the canoe was tied up, they saw smoke rising from a cheerful campfire, the two small tents pitched nearby. Ian was some distance away, propped up against cushions from the canoe.

Carol didn't disturb him, but set to work preparing the food. A green bamboo pole served as a spit on which to cook the pheasant; she steamed the asparagus in a wrapping of thick leaves, and roasted the yams in the embers.

When all was ready she went to inform Ian. He was staring pensively at the stars, which were beginning to appear.

"Dinner is served, my lord," she announced in a humble tone, trying to suppress the smile of triumph on her face. "Would the master care to carve the pheasant?"

Ian rose without a word and came over to where Carol had laid out the dinner. With a great show of chivalry he ushered Carol onto one of the cushions he had brought and then proceeded solemnly to carve the steaming bird with Jutai's knife, serving first Carol, who dutifully waited although she was now ravenous, and then Jutai and then himself.

As they started eating Carol waited anxiously for his verdict. The silence of night was broken only by the crackling of the fire and the rhythmical croaking of frogs on the river bank.

At last he pronounced his judgment. "The asparagus is delicious, but where's the hollandaise sauce?"

His face was deadpan as he said it, but his ludicrous comment broke the tension that had existed between them since her accident in the boat. She broke into gales of laughter. Ian joined in the mirth with a mock scolding that the pheasant would also have tasted better stuffed with herbs.

"Herbs?" said Jutai interrupting his contented chewing on a leg. "Many good herbs here in the forest. Next time I find herbs for dinner, too."

Carol sensed that the Indian was a little put out because she was receiving the credit for the meal. She hoped he would forgive her—tonight she needed Ian's approval more than he did.

She attempted to mollify Jutai's hurt feelings by praising his skill as a herbalist. "Dr. Todd tells me that you make a successful love potion too, Jutai."

Jutai nodded. "Yes, love potion very good. Make fierce man tender lover." Looking from Ian to Carol and back again with a smirk on his face, he added, "Maybe Señor Morrison should try some."

"I don't need it, Jutai," said Ian with a sigh. "Or perhaps I've taken some without knowing it. I seem to be suffering from its poisonous effects."

Carol had to admit to herself that if sexual attraction was all that was needed to turn a man's head, Juanita had the ability to hand out liberal doses of love potion. "Possibly the lady has given you some," she said.

"The lady I'm talking about doesn't need to resort to witchcraft," he replied. "She weaves her own spell."

"Or her dressmaker does," put in Carol, trying her best not to sound cutting. "Clothes help, you know."

"No, it's not her clothes, although she does look good in them, especially green. It's her vivacity, her resourcefulness, her sense of humor— She makes me feel very young and alive."

Carol couldn't remember Juanita exhibiting much of a sense of humor, but then of course she didn't know her very well. She was certainly vivacious, and she could be considered resourceful in that she had discovered how to disguise her short stature and make the most of her voluptuous figure. Ian had also once told Carol that he liked poise in a woman; Juanita was not only poised, she was ultrasophisticated.

It was unfortunate that Ian had switched the conversation to Juanita, although Carol had come to accept that his sweetheart was never far from his thoughts, except when he was immersed in his medical work. This evening, mellowed by his strenuous day and full of good food, no wonder he was pining for his absent lady-love. It seemed a bit unfair all the same, considering that it was Carol who had prepared his supper. Quite irrationally she experienced a pang of jealousy for Juanita . . . then quickly banished the uncharitable thoughts from her mind. She cared nothing for Juanita, and all she wanted from Ian for herself was respect, respect as a capable partner and as a woman.

With that assurance running through her head, she stood up and said that she was tired and would like to go to bed.

"You take that tent," Ian instructed her, pointing to the one nearer the fire. "It can get quite cold during the night. I'll use the other one. Jutai sleeps under the stars—he's used to it."

"I keep fire burning," Jutai volunteered. "Then animals stay away. Not dangerous, but might scare nurse-lady."

Carol glanced around at the bushes surrounding the clearing, now no more than dark silhouettes under the moonless sky. Pairs of unblinking eyes reflected the fire's glow. She was relieved to know that Jutai would be keeping watch.

"Good night, then," she said.

"Good night, Carol," said Ian. "And thanks very much for the dinner." He touched her cheek with his finger tips to emphasize his gratitude, and she felt the spot tingling as the charm of his touch again had that extraordinary effect on her pulse. Like a silly schoolgirl might have reacted, it flashed into her mind whether he would have kissed her it Jutai hadn't been there. Worse, the fantasy of him embracing her persisted, growing in intensity until she could almost feel the pressure of his mouth on hers. Embarrassed, she turned quickly to retreat into the seclusion of her tiny tent.

Daybreak next morning found the campers already loading up their canoe. Although she had at the time welcomed Ian's decision to stop for the night, Carol now felt refreshed and keen to finish their onerous journey. Every hour counted for the Indians who had already been in contact with one of the measles cases.

With renewed vigor they paddled upstream, manipulating obstructions and maneuvering the boat past shallow places, until at last the creek widened sufficiently to give them clear passage. They put on a spurt of speed and arrived at the crudely built dock that served the village of Pucallpa before Carol's watch showed nine o'clock. Scores of curious natives watched them land.

Ian was pleased to find that the instructions he had sent through Jutai's cousin Mono had been carried out. The head man of the village, the most dazzling of all in his straw wig and feathers, had overruled the local witch doctor's prescription of hot irons to the measles rashes and had isolated the eight cases, six of whom were babies. The villagers had buried the two old men who had died, but there was no evidence of public mourning—it appeared they had been on their last legs anyway.

Using Jutai as interpreter, Ian was told that the population of the village was about four hundred, including satellite settlements farther up the creek. Another hundred lived out in the bush within a couple hours' walking distance.

"Not as many as I thought," he said to Carol. "If you get started with the immunization right away while I'm attending the sick, we should have the whole village inoculated by this evening. And the head man will send runners to the outlying areas to bring the rest in for treatment early tomorrow morning. We'll be finished by morning coffee time and able to get back to Iquitos tomorrow night, taking the new data for my research study with us."

"Coffee time?" Carol's eyes opened wide with anticipation. "You mean they have coffee here? I'd love a cup before we start. We haven't had any breakfast, you know."

"Of course they don't have coffee," he laughed deridingly. "I was only kidding. Jutai will arrange for a slab of cassava bread and some fruit juice if you're hungry, but be quick about it; I want you at work in fifteen minutes."

Carol munched at her piece of doughy bread and

washed it down with mango juice while waiting for the sterilizer to boil. In less than her allotted fifteen minutes she was hard at work, injecting the lifesaving serum into the arms of a long line of Indians. As with the villagers at the camp, the first recipients were reluctant to come forward, but with persuasion by Jutai they were soon pressing around in an almost unmanageable throng. Carol had to keep refilling her syringe and changing needles at lightning speed to keep up with the demand for her services.

Her only really unwilling patient was the local witch doctor. When the head man had received his own shot, he forcibly held forward the medicine man's arm to the jeers of the crowd. Afterward she caught sight of him sulking in a corner of the compound where she had set up shop—his pride had obviously been badly wounded. She hoped he wouldn't take his revenge by casting some dreadful hex on her.

She expressed her fears to Jutai during a brief lull in her work. But Jutai was unconcerned. "That man nothing," he said. "He not harm nurse-lady. But tonight he put on a big dance-show to make people believe in him again."

So the witch doctor would have a chance to regain the confidence of the village by performing some impressive dances this evening. She hoped she would be allowed to watch. She might pick up some tips herself on keeping patients happy.

A new batch of patients arrived in time to prevent further ruminations. They mobbed around her makeshift treatment table, and she had to work continuously for the next three hours to keep the waiting crowd from becoming restless. Then after a short pause for another piece of bread, another drink of mango juice, she got to her feet and carried on again until her arms ached and her brain became fuddled.

The hands on her watch pointed to six, and the shadows across the compound were beginning to lengthen before she had dealt with the last of the stragglers and Jutai had announced that the entire village had been inoculated. Closing her eyes she collapsed her exhausted body on a

84

convenient log—her work was done for the day. All she wanted now was a cooling shower, some pretty, clean clothes, and for someone to congratulate her. The first two, she knew, were out of the question, but the appreciation wouldn't cost anything.

"Hello, Carol, taking a breather?" was Ian's first remark when he came up.

"No, I've finished. Every last one of them," she replied.

"Well done. I've finished my rounds, too. You look a bit pooped. I think we deserve a drink after that. Come on, we'll go and sit down by the stream." His praise wasn't quite as effusive as she thought she deserved, but even a morsel is food for the starving, and the invitation to join him for a drink was an improvement over the usual master-slave relationship.

He led her to a quiet spot on the bank of a gurgling stream at the edge of the village. A huge flowering jacaranda tree provided shade and something to lean against. For both of them to use the trunk as a backrest, they had to sit close together, elbows touching. Ian seemed as unmoved by the contact as if they had been passengers on a bus, but she found herself acutely conscious of it, and, when he pressed hard against her to reach into his pocket for a hip flask, a shiver of expectation ran up her spine, and she caught her breath sharply.

He unscrewed the flask and passed it to her. "Here, have some brandy. It'll put you in the right mood for the feast and the entertainment to come."

Carol took a sip and passed it back, noticing with pleasure that he put it to his own lips without wiping it. Not hygienic perhaps, but delightfully intimate. "Jutai said there was going to be some dancing. The local witch doctor appears to be the star."

"That's right. It's to celebrate the exorcism of the evil spirit that brought the white man's disease to the village. Naturally the witch doctor has to see that he gets the credit."

"While we who did the work sit by and watch?"

He smiled at her and patted her knee—a simple gesture of sympathy, but it made her leg muscles tighten and her heart beat a little faster— "Don't be jealous, Carol. He has to save face. These witch doctors are a menace unless they become converted like Jutai; then they can be very useful because they have authority."

"How are they trained?" she asked. "Are they licensed or anything?"

"The only training they get is from the one before them. That's how their nonsense gets passed on. Talking of medical licenses, my Peruvian one is up for renewal very soon. Without it I wouldn't be allowed to go on working here as a doctor. I hope it goes through all right."

"Why shouldn't it? Everyone knows you're doing great work."

"It has to be granted by the minister of health in Lima. And the minister of health happens to be Ricardo Muñoz's uncle. That's why I'm indebted to the Muñozes. They helped me originally."

The significance of this fact was lost on Carol at first. "That should make it easy then. . . ."

"It did when I first came here. Ricardo and I were friends then. But things have changed in the last little while." Ian twisted his head to look deep into Carol's eyes, an expression of sadness and inevitability in his own gray orbs. He sighed and slowly shook his head, as though she were in some way responsible for Ian's problem with his license. She didn't understand.

"Why have you and Ricardo fallen out? It's not anything to do with me, is it? I know he's been making passes at me, but . . ." A sudden thought struck her. "Ian, I'll try and be nicer to him if it would help you . . ."

He jumped as though stung by a bee. "Don't you dare!" he barked. "I don't want you to have anything to do with the wretched man. He . . . he betrayed a trust, that's all I can tell you. Stay away from him. You must, Carol, I insist on it!"

His vehemence alarmed her, and also annoyed her a little. Here was Ian giving her orders again, orders that had nothing to do with her work, intruding himself into her private life in the way she had determined to resist.

"I've told you before," she said. "It's impossible for me

86

to ignore him altogether when I'm a guest in his house. But I'll try to avoid any repetition of that incident with his father's butterflies—for my own sake as much as yours."

Ian's only comment was to mutter under his breath, "You'd better." He took another draught from his flask, and a tense silence descended between them.

Another idea came to Carol. "But surely Juanita has some influence with her uncle, too. That should help as far as getting your license is concerned. I mean, after all, you two . . ."

His temper still hadn't subsided. "Just leave Juanita out of this, will you! She's nothing whatever to do with you . . ."

"All right, all right," she said resignedly. Nothing she could say seemed to please him this afternoon. It seemed best to forget the whole thing. She clambered to her feet. "I think I'll go and get some rest before this feast begins. Where am I to sleep, do you know?"

Ian snapped out of the reverie into which he had sunk. "Sleep? Oh yes, we've been given that hut there behind us. I've asked them to rig up a piece of coconut matting between us. It'll be more comfortable than in the tents. And safer from insects."

The hut had been furnished with two straw mattresses and a large sheet of matting strung between them. Apart from that there were only bare boards and a window without glass on each side. Like all the jungle buildings it was raised off the ground on stilts, and a verandah had been built outside the entrance, affording a pleasant view of the stream they had been sitting by.

With a last glance at Ian, still sitting moodily under the jacaranda tree, Carol went inside and threw herself on the mattress, which hadn't got Ian's medical bag beside it. All her weariness had returned, accentuated by the glow of brandy inside her. She closed her eyes and tried to forget the unpredictable man who was to share her accommodation for the night.

Only seconds later, it seemed, she opened them to see him standing in the entrance, holding back the curtain, looking at her. Embarrassed, she got up off the bed.

"I must have dropped off," she said. "How long have you been there?"

"Only a minute. I hate to wake you—you looked so peaceful there—but Jutai has come to tell us that the feast and the dancing are about to begin. If we miss it, we won't get anything to eat tonight—unless you want to go hunting again." He was grinning now; his bad mood had evaporated as quickly as it had come.

With Jutai leading the way, they made their way through the village to the compound where Carol had worked that afternoon. Darkness had fallen, but their path was lit by flaming torches being carried by some of the men to the accompaniment of beating drums and curious, tuneless chanting. The flickering light cast eerie shadows on the houses and on the excited mob of Indians as they walked or ran, all converging on the central compound.

Carol wasn't exactly frightened, but she took Ian's arm to make sure they weren't jostled apart. He pressed her hand to his side, and she immediately felt comfortable and secure.

Jutai indicated to them that they should sit in a certain place on the ground near the head man and his family while he himself chose a spot farther away to squat with his cousin Mono. The head man nodded gruffly at them, but the local witch doctor, attired now in magnificent regalia, avoided their look of recognition.

Women brought food and set it before them. A whole, wild boar, steaming in the light of the torches, was torn apart by the head man himself, and the pieces passed to his seated guests. Flat loaves of cassava bread were devoured with equal relish as well as some appetizing nuts and fruit, each person unceremoniously seizing what he wanted for himself. Carol noted that even the small children were dipping shells into a central bowl of opaque white liquid and sipping from them. Ian explained that this was manioc, the unsanitary native brew—fortunately, nobody pressed him and Carol to partake also.

Instead he gave her several draughts from his brandy flask. "I brought this along for medicinal purposes," he said with a wink.

"You also brought *me* along for working purposes," she rejoined, "but, like the brandy, I'm good for other purposes, too."

"I don't know what you mean by that," he said, a surprised look on his face.

She didn't quite know what she had meant by it either—the words had just slipped out. Fortunately she didn't have to try and explain, as a furious beating of drums and mournful wails of several primitive wind instruments suddenly rent the night air. The entertainment was ready to start. The noisy crowd behind them, who had been milling about the compound while the head man's guests ate their meal, fell into awed silence. A row of torchbearers marked off the square that was to be the stage. Carol leaned forward expectantly, craning her neck for a better view.

The witch doctor rose to his feet and strode to center stage, arms held high like an actor acknowledging applause. But there was no applause—only a few titters and some shouted words, which brought laughter from the crowd. He was going to have to work hard to restore his reputation tonight. But, quite unfazed, he turned and took a great leap into the air, a bloodcurdling yell coming from his mouth. The crowd gasped, and Carol held her breath, as the man made two more gigantic twists in the air, his feathered head-dress thrown back and his arms flailing in demonic abandon.

Here one of the musicians let out a slow, low-pitched sound. "That's the barkhorn," Ian whispered. "It incarnates evil spirits." Sure enough, a figure in a black cloak, his face white with chalk, slunk into the arena and made menacing, deathlike gestures. The audience cringed in fear. "The white man's disease," said Ian. "Now you know what we're up against with our serum."

The pantomime went into a more subdued, lyrical phase with the arrival of a comely girl who swayed her grass skirt in front of the witch doctor. He responded to her advances with enthusiasm, dancing wildly round her in demonstration of his prowess, while the evil spirit skulked in the background, casting his hand over some lesser characters who had ventured onto the stage. Each in turn reacted with tortured movements and eventual collapse to the ground.

"The naughty doctor is dallying with his girlfriend while the epidemic spreads," Ian explained. "Dereliction of duty, I call it."

"But understandable," said Carol. "She's very pretty."

Now another figure appeared, also a woman, brandishing a length of bamboo, which Carol recognized as a blowgun similar to the one Jutai had used to shoot the pheasant. She danced around the witch doctor, apparently trying to attract his attention away from the first girl, gesticulating despondently at the carnage being wrought by the devil-man. From time to time she blew a few imaginary darts at the evil one herself, but he only laughed as they hit his body, continuing his wave of destruction.

"They don't think much of their nurses in this village," Carol whispered.

"They're not enlightened like we are," grinned Ian.

At last the second woman succeeded in diverting the amorous witch doctor's attention to the evil spirit. He snatched the bamboo from her and, with deadly accuracy, fired again and again at the monster, who reeled from each impact with a terrible cry of pain, as the flutes in the orchestra whined—"They represent the incarnation of good spirits," said Ian—and the drums beat to a crescendo. The crowd was going mad with excitement now, and when the hero, assisted by the girl who kept handing him fresh darts, finally slew the killer, he accepted their adulation with a spectacular show of triumphant dancing.

As a finale, he pushed aside his original girlfriend when she ran up to reclaim him after his tremendous feat and danced a passionate duet with his nurse instead.

"That's a new twist," said Carol. "Not true to life at all."

"Oh, I don't know," replied Ian, rubbing his chin and not looking at her while he spoke. "Some guys can't keep their business separated from their pleasure. I'm glad I'm not like that."

The couple on the stage were now rubbing noses in an

unusual form of embrace while the corpse of the evil spirit lay writhing in a death-throe at their feet. The other girl had fled from the scene altogether. The crowd, recognizing the end of the performance, broke through the cordon of torchbearers to swarm around the witch doctor and his partner. The people sitting near Ian and Carol scrambled to their feet and joined in the pandemonium.

"Come on, let's get out of here," said Ian, taking Carol by the hand, "They've all drunk a lot of manioc, and anything might happen. It's not us they're crazy about. They will actually believe that *he* saved the village from measles now. He's a real showman. We better make ourselves scarce. He might just turn them against us."

"Surely he's got better sense than that," said Carol as they picked their way unheeded through the seething mass of grass-skirted villagers. "He's no fool. He knows he may need you again to save his reputation."

"I guess you're right," Ian agreed. They had reached the outskirts of the crowd now and were walking through a quiet street toward the hut where they were to spend the night. Ian still held her hand, and she made no move to let it go.

A full moon was peeping over the top of the forest and sparkling on the stream when they arrived at their hut. From the village could be heard the distant throbbing of drums. The sound of the waterfall was temptingly close. And there was not a soul in sight. But none of this seemed to have any effect on Ian. At the top of the steps leading up to their verandah, he released Carol's hand and went ahead of her through the entrance to disappear behind the curtain into his own half of the room.

"I'll help you with the inoculations tomorrow morning," he called. "We'll do them somewhere more private than the compound. After tonight's frenzy it would be more tactful. Be ready to start early so that we can be on our way down to the camp as soon as possible. Good night."

Mr. Cold Efficiency, sighed Carol to herself. No sooner do I think he's warming up than he retreats back into his shell. I suppose he's missing Juanita again after two nights without her. Well, she can have him as far as I'm concerned. And I'm not concerned—not concerned one little bit.

She took off all her clothes except the long shirt she was wearing under the safari suit and stretched out on the mattress. Only a few feet away she could hear Ian grunt as he pulled off his boots—a moment later his mattress rustled and the hut became silent. It was disturbing to think that he was lying just the other side of that flimsy partition, probably as undressed as she was. They had been through a lot together in the last two days. She admired him enormously, and *he* liked *her*, too, she told herself, since she had found her feet in this alien environment. A man and a woman, partners and friends, miles from anywhere, separated by a piece of rotten old coconut matting! It seemed an awful waste.

The moon climbed higher and shafted through the window above her onto her bare legs, giving them a silver brilliance. She wiggled her toes playfully, and the light reflected from her nail polish. What was the matter with her? She should be dead tired by this hour, but she wasn't. She wanted to get up and do something. Something naughty, something exciting . . .

She slid noiselessly off the mattress and stood up. Ian's heavy breathing indicated that he was already asleep. She tiptoed across the floor and peeked round the curtain. He was flat on his back, stripped to the waist, his hair tousled and his features relaxed. He looked very young asleep . . . and vulnerable. A guilty feeling crept over her for watching him this way, but he had done it to her that very afternoon, hadn't he? She wondered whether he had been thinking then what she was thinking now—whether he had also felt drawn to the bedside, whether the same sort of fanciful ideas had occurred to him as were now racing through her unruly brain.

Stop it! she whispered aloud to herself, you must be going out of your mind. Pull yourself together before you do something you'll regret tomorrow.

She stepped back from the curtain, but sleep would be impossible for a while yet. She felt far too stimulated for that. She tiptoed out onto the verandah. The tantalizing sound of the waterfall came to her ears. A cool shower, that was what she wanted, a cool shower in the moonlight to wash away the cares of the day . . .

The smooth, glittering rocks on the stream bed felt delicious under her bare feet, and the bubbling water swirled teasingly around her ankles as she waded up to the waterfall. It cascaded down into a shallow pool, every drop of foam shining silver, like stars, against the lush dark green of the foliage all around.

She took off her shirt and laid it out of reach of the spray—then plunged into the glorious refreshment of the pool. The tumbling water splashed onto her head, sending her hair streaming over her face. Happily she played in it, laughing like a lttle girl, until the water and her seemed to merge . . . it was over her, and under her, and in her. Finally she climbed out and sat on a rock, her head thrown back to the star-filled sky above, wide-eyed with pleasure, her only regret being that she had nobody to share the delightful experience with.

In the warm air her skin soon dried enough for her to be able to pull her shirt on again. Slowly she made her way back down the stream. She was almost opposite the hut before she saw Ian standing on the bank watching her. She put her hand to her mouth to suppress a cry and then clutched vainly at the damp, clinging shirt around her breasts and thighs.

He observed her attempts at modesty without apparent emotion before saying quietly, "I told you not to walk around here in bare feet."

"I . . . I forgot. I wanted to cool off."

"Come here. I'll carry you back to the hut. The muddy bank is the worst place for foot-worms. Walking will get you bilharziasis for sure."

She took a few unsteady paces toward him, and then he lifted her effortlessly into his arms. Automatically her arms went around his neck and her wet hair clung to his face and bare shoulder. The clammy shirt was no barrier between her chest and his—she felt free and uncluttered and brazenly joyful as he carried her away.

Giggling, she kicked her long, slim legs in the air. She

didn't care what he thought of her nuzzling against the dark curls of his chest, she didn't care what happened next, she didn't care about anything except this fabulous sensation of being in heaven!

By the time they reached the hut her heart was beating wildly, and she could feel his thumping too, though whether it was from the exertion or for the same reason as her own commotion she couldn't tell.

He took her inside and laid her on the bed, studying the entire length of her barely-covered body with ill-concealed approval. She looked up at him and giggled again.

"You're a bad, bad girl," he said softly. A smile broke onto his face, his crinkly eyes glinting in the moonlight. "Now go to sleep and don't bother me any more."

He vanished behind the curtain, and all was quiet again in the room. But it was a long time before his heavy breathing started up again, and it was even longer before sleep finally took over from the glorious fantasy in which she reveled after he was gone.

Chapter 5

Antonio's motor boat touched the jetty in Iquitos at dusk the next evening. The three days that Carol and Ian had been away seemed like a lifetime to her. So much had happened; such changes had taken place within her.

There had been almost no time for conversation since early morning. She and Ian had quickly disposed of the immunization of the Indians who had come into Pucallpa the night before from outlying settlements. Then, with Jutai again in the bow of the canoe, they had paddled all day down the creek to Dr. Todd's camp.

Ian had immediately summoned Antonio to make ready

the motorboat. While waiting on the dock he had said casually to Henry Todd, "I'm looking forward to seeing my honey again," to which Henry had answered, "I'm sure you are. She'll have missed you, too." Carol had offered no comment; she suspected that Ian's remark was designed to put her in her place after her behavior last night. She felt herself blushing at the reminiscence, but at the same time smiling for the sheer joy of it. Nothing would ever be quite the same again between her and her boss—for that she wasn't sorry.

It took a few minutes to start the jeep after three days of disuse, and Carol noted Ian's mounting impatience. Glancing at his watch as he revved up the engine, he muttered to himself, "I should have brought her a present after being away so long." Then they sped away down the road to the Muñoz villa. At the top of the driveway he told her, "Hop out here. I'll see you later." Abruptly he drove off, just as he had on a previous occasion when he had dropped her off on the way back from the camp.

Every two or three days a new present, thought Carol. It's just as well he's a rich man. I wonder what she does with all the things he brings her. Idly casts them on one side, I expect.

Ricardo came bustling into the entrance hall at the sound of her closing the front door behind her. "Ah, there you are, Carol. I was worried about you. Are you sure you're all right?"

"Just fine, thank you. Why shouldn't I be?"

"Well, we got Ian's message, and it seemed to us most unfair of him to make you go all that way into the jungle."

"That's what I'm here for," Carol replied cheerfully, "to immunize the Indians. Besides, I enjoyed it."

Ricardo was looking her up and down. "You look stunning in that outfit," he said, appreciative eyes following her curves.

"I'm looking forward to getting out of it just the same. If you'll excuse me, I'll go up and change . . ."

Carol was starting up the stairs when Juanita came into the hall. "Why did you go on that trip with Ian?" she spat. "He had no business taking you."

Carol looked down at her from her vantage point on the staircase. "Because he wanted me to. I'm meant to work with him, you know. He could never have managed it alone."

Juanita uttered a snort of disgust. "Where is he anyway? Why isn't he here?"

"I believe he's out buying you a gift if you want to know. I would think you'd be grateful." With that she turned and continued up the stairs, as erect and dignified as she could, considering the stiffness in her joints after a whole day's paddling.

Newly washed hair, clean linen slacks, and a pretty little peasant blouse felt marvelous after her working clothes, however much Ricardo admired them. With a twinkle she pushed the sleeves of the blouse off her shoulders before going down to dinner. She wanted to look as feminine to Ian as possible tonight, as a contrast to the intrepid explorer look he had already seen too much of.

Talk at dinner was dreary. The hostility between Ian and Ricardo showed clearly. Ian gave a brief description of the Indian dance they had witnessed at Pulcallpa—and Ricardo commented with the one word "savages" under his breath. Ricardo also made a pointed remark about Carol deserving a day off after her strenuous trip—a suggestion with which Carol heartily agreed—and Ian muttered that there was still a lot of work to be done at the camp. Juanita ate her spiced beef in silence. Only Carol herself was in buoyant spirits. Although Ian avoided talking to her directly, she had noticed his eyes light up when she had come into the room. The fact that Ricardo's eyes had shone like beacons, too, was immaterial.

At length Juanita brought up the subject of an important wedding to which the Muñoz brother and sister had been invited the following Saturday evening. She did so hope Ian would accompany them. He would enjoy meeting some of their friends, and the delicious banquet afterward. Ian demurred, saying that he never enjoyed himself at weddings.

"But, Ian," Juanita pressed him, "you've never been to a Peruvian wedding. You should get some experience of

96

one. There's a lot of interesting ritual you should know about."

Before you have to go through one yourself, thought Carol ruefully.

"I think Carol should come, too," Ricardo announced as though she had no choice in the matter. "I'll phone the bride's mother tomorrow. She'll be pleased to send the invitations."

The idea appealed to Carol, especially if Ian could be persuaded to come. "What does one wear to a Peruvian wedding?" she asked.

"Your best evening dress," said Ricardo. "This will be an opportunity for you to look even more ravishing than you do tonight."

Juanita coughed. "You will come, won't you, Ian?" she pleaded, resting a well-manicured hand on his arm.

"I'll think about it," said Ian. "I suppose it is Saturday night, and I wasn't planning on going up to the camp on Sunday."

And so the matter was left when Carol went discreetly up to her room after the coffee. In a drawer of her dressing table she came across the black orchid Ian had given to her. It had dried somewhat, but still retained the vibrant sheen of the fresh blossom. Carefully she arranged its petals so that they would lie flat and inserted it between the pages of the book she had been reading. Then she put the book in her closet with the weight of her suitcase on top of it. The beauty of the orchid would now be preserved for as long as she wanted to keep it.

The rest of the week passed. Every morning she and Ian would go up to the camp, and every evening come back down to the villa for a dinner of desultory chat with Ricardo and Juanita. Afterward Carol always retired to bed before the others. Ricardo didn't make any overt advances toward her, although once she spotted him following her up the stairs. She threw a stern "Good *night*, Ricardo," over her shoulder at him and noisily bolted her door behind her, which apparently was enough to deter him from knocking.

Sometimes she would hear Ian's operatic records wafting up from the living room and deliberately shut her mind to the image they conjured up. During the day he was much more polite than he had been at first, but she sensed a certain reserve in his attitude, and any allusion to their trip to Pucallpa was brushed aside with a cool smile and a change of topic. Most of the time she worked by herself inoculating more of the Indians from the many communities around the camp, not even having Henry Todd for company during lunch, for the old man had not been feeling well lately and spent most of his time on his bunk. Ian never joined her for lunch either. She assumed he worked straight through the day.

She allowed herself little time to think about her feelings toward Ian. Right after he had carried her to her bed that night, she had imagined herself possessed by him, consumed with desire. Never before had she thrown herself at a man like that, exposing the raw ends of her deepest sensibilities. It had been a novel, and, she had to admit, intoxicating experience.

Now that the tempo of their life together had slowed to the verge of routine, she had only one word for her feelings—confused. She was happy to be near him, she was worried about what his life with Juanita would be like after they were married, and she tried not to think about what her life would be like after she had left Iquitos, and him, forever.

Saturday came at last. Ian had decided to go to the wedding, and both he and Carol had graciously accepted the engraved invitations that had arrived a few days before. At two o'clock in the afternoon he sauntered up to where Carol was working with the news that they were taking the rest of the day off. "To give you plenty of time to titivate," he said. "The cream of Iquitos will be there tonight. I want my nurse looking her best."

"I'll try not to let you down. But what about Ricardo? What I'd like to wear might overstimulate him."

"Don't worry about that. *I'll* handle Ricardo if he gets out of line." Ian's jaw set firmly. With him as her bodyguard, Carol knew she would be safe.

When she went up to change for the wedding and the

banquet, Carol had already long before decided to wear her backless blue silk dress. Her auburn hair, lighter now after days in the sunshine, hung loose, framing her face. She chose a darker, more alluring, make-up than usual and accentuated her eyes with shadow and mascara until the natural radiance with which they shone these days was exaggerated into brilliance. With pleasure she found that the neckline of her halter top plunged lower than she remembered. As she assessed her appearance in the mirror, she decided that she had never looked so glamorous in her life.

The quartet set off in Ricardo's large black limousine. Both men were dressed in tuxedos, Ian's suit fitting him in that same casual way as his white one did, while Ricardo's stretched tightly across his waistband. Juanita was in green brocade—hadn't Ian said he liked her in green?—flowing about her ankles.

The service in the cathedral was inspiring in its pomp. A full choir sang in well-practiced harmony after the bishop had pronounced the young couple man and wife. Then the bride, smiling serenely, walked slowly down the aisle on the arm of her stern-faced bridegroom, watched by every one of the hundreds of guests.

A lump formed in Carol's throat. Weddings didn't usually affect her that way, but this one in Iquitos Cathedral did . . . was it because this scene would be repeated not long hence with the two people standing on her right as the principals? Undoubtedly Juanita was having the same thoughts; she was gazing up at Ian's profile with a gleam in her eye. He, however, was staring straight ahead into space, almost unaware of the moving scenario on his left.

The postnuptial banquet was held in the ballroom of the *ayuntamiento,* the ornate, yellow brick town hall, which had once been a Spanish palace. Ricardo drove them there and parked in the adjoining city square. They joined the stream of worthy citizens, all dressed in evening clothes, across the elegantly laid out gardens, in through the huge open door to the ballroom. Glittering glass chandeliers hung from the frescoed ceiling, and great somber portraits lined the walls.

Dutifully they filed through the reception line and then made their way to the buffet table along one wall. Carol helped herself from the bewildering array of delicacies, sticking to those she recognized. Lobster, baby sausages, canapés, salad, and mayonnaise all heaped onto her plate.

Ricardo turned away from the buffet at the same time as she did. "We'll go to that table over there," he directed her.

"Let's wait for Ian and Juanita," she replied, turning back.

But Juanita had other plans. "Darling," she was saying to Ian, "I've arranged an invitation for us to sit with the governor of the province and his wife. You must meet him; he's very important."

"I'd rather we all stayed together," said Ian.

"Oh, we can't, darling. The governor only invited us two, and it would be terribly rude to turn him down. Let's go." Juanita started leading Ian across the room.

He gave Carol a shrug of helplessness, and she smiled back at him reassuringly. It was all right; Ricardo couldn't get up to anything in this crowded room.

Ricardo and Carol sat at a large circular table where most of the seats were already occupied by portly ladies and gentlemen tucking into their food and talking garrulously in Spanish.

Their plates were almost empty, and they had drunk several glasses of champagne when Ricardo leaned toward her confidentially. "Carol, it has distressed me terribly that you have been living in my house for nearly two weeks, and we've had so little time together. There are so many things I've longed to show you, but that Ian keeps you working like a slave . . ."

"I'm not on holiday, you know," she said.

"That's the sad thing about it," he replied. "I think you should be on holiday. Why don't you resign your job and stay on as my guest? We could have the most marvelous time together. I could take you everywhere . . ."

"It's very sweet of you, Ricardo, but I'm afraid that's impossible. I have a job to do, an important job with the Indians. . . ."

"Indians!" he spat, throwing an arm into the air in dismissal of the whole Indian race. "How many Indians do you see in this room? Now listen, my dearest Carol. I have many friends in and around Iquitos, men with vast *ranchos* and fishing lodges. You could ride, you could hunt, you could play tennis, you could live the life a beautiful girl like you should be living, instead of grubbing in the dirt with a lot of Indians for a brutal master . . ."

"Ian is not brutal," she said with vehemence. "And any idea of my quitting my job is out of the question."

Ricardo looked downcast. "Well, in that case . . . How long will your work last, Carol?"

"About three more weeks, I should think. Why?"

"Then why not stay on after it is over and let me give you the holiday you so well deserve?"

"I'll see," she hedged. "I'll probably have to go straight back to the States."

"Three weeks! I can't wait so long!" cried Ricardo, pounding his fist into his forehead. "You don't understand, Carol. I have . . . important plans for us both, but we must get to know each other better before I can even discuss them." Carol stared at him in amazement, but he placed a pudgy hand on hers in a tender gesture she hadn't the heart to snub by withdrawing, and went on, "Yes, it's true, my dearest, I have plans . . . wonderful plans . . . but let us talk about the present. Tomorrow is your day off, I believe. That tyrant you work for . . ."

"Now stop that talk, or I'll go away," she cut in.

"All right. But at least let me take you out tomorrow. One day is so little, but it would whet your appetite for more, I feel certain. Say you will come." His appealing look would have been comical if he hadn't been so obviously sincere.

Carol remembered what Marilyn had told her about Ricardo losing his fiancée last year, and she couldn't help but feel sorry for him. At least his intentions appeared to be honorable, which might make him easier to keep under control. Besides, she couldn't think of a valid excuse not to go with him tomorrow. But Ian wouldn't be working tomorrow either, and she would infinitely rather go somewhere with *him*. . . . But that was absurd; of course he would be spending the day with Juanita. Carol decided to temporize again.

"I won't promise anything, Ricardo. Ask me in the morning."

"Ah, you make me happy at last!" he beamed, as if she had already accepted his invitation. "I will show you how a *real* man should treat a girl like you . . ."

Carol was about to carry out her threat and leave the table at this low-down reference to Ian, but someone came up on Ricardo's other side, slapping him on the shoulder and immediately engaging him in a voluble conversation in Spanish. This was the moment when she could slip away without Ricardo making a scene. While his back was turned to her, she quietly rose from her chair and made her way between the tables to the door into the garden. She was a tiny bit dizzy from the champagne and from Ricardo's persistent pressure, and the prospect of some fresh air seemed good.

The garden was cool and quiet after the noisy ballroom. Clouds drifted across the moon so that it was nearly dark, but she saw a fountain ahead of her and walked slowly down to the little flagstone courtyard that surrounded it. She took a cigarette from her handbag and inhaled gratefully, listening to the traffic moving round the square and the buzz of voices from the banquet.

"Smoking again?" said Ian's voice behind her. "What awful things are you expecting to happen this time?"

"I certainly wasn't expecting *you*," she said, the smile on her face revealing her pleasure at his intrusion. "I thought you were hobnobbing with the governor."

"I slipped out while he was regaling Juanita with a long story about his latest crocodile hunt. Actually I saw you come out here and I wondered what was up. Is Ricardo pestering you?"

"No, not really." She didn't want to talk about Ricardo. "Crocodiles, eh? Do you remember that ugly beast we saw on our way to Pucallpa? It scared the life out of me."

"I remember a lot of things about Pucallpa. That beautiful pheasant dinner for one thing."

"Ah, the way to a man's heart is through his stomach," she laughed, "I always knew it."

"The way to *my* heart . . ." he said, and stopped. "Yes, your cooking was a great deal better than the so-called feast the next night. You're good at quite a variety of things, aren't you?" He had moved a little closer now and was looking down into her eyes. Her heart skipped a beat, and her lips parted slightly.

"Thank you, sir," she said coyly.

"Did you like the way the witchdoctor and his nurse rubbed noses at the end of the dance?"

"I can think of better ways for him to show his appreciation."

"I agree. Our way is more fun, isn't it?"

She nodded, half-expectant, half-afraid, knowing what was coming next.

Caution flew to the winds as he took her in his arms. His hands slid firmly across the bare skin of her back, sending a shiver down her spine. He drew her toward him, molding her body to his. She arched her back, raising her face to meet his mouth, waiting for the ecstatic moment when he would kiss her. Suddenly he pressed down hard on her lips, fiercely, relentlessly. She felt every sinew in his body tighten while she herself went limp. This was not the soft, tender brushing of lips on lips that he had stolen at the party last week—this was passion and unrestrained desire, and she capitulated totally to it for a full minute . . .

Then the glorious moment of the embrace turned to horror at what she saw over his hunched shoulder. Calmly surveying them was the unmistakable shadow of Juanita, standing in the light of the ballroom door, not twenty feet away.

Carol's flaccid muscles tautened into terrified rigidity as she fought to free herself from him. Pushing against his chest with all her strength, she wrenched her mouth from his, and stood panting, twisting in his powergrip.

"You . . . you don't want me!" he blurted, shocked, incredulous and angry. "You've been playing with me. . . . Why, you rotten tease!"

She broke away at last and fled across the lawn, his voice ringing in her ears. "I'll never forgive you for this . . . never!"

Tears streaming down her face, sobs choking her until she could hardly breathe, Carol ran out of the garden, across the road, and into the public square. She fell into the back seat of the nearest taxi and managed to say, "Casa del Corona" to the astonished driver before burying her head in her hands and letting out a long, low wail like a wounded animal.

Even in the locked confines of her room, Carol found it hard to think clearly. It had all happened so quickly—the magic of Ian's kiss, which had turned her body to water, the awful reminder from Juanita that she was trespassing on forbidden ground, and, to cap it all, Ian's misunderstanding of why she had fled.

She lay sprawled on her bed, dress and hair in disarray, mascara streaks on her face, whimpering into the stillness . . .

Gradually the events came into focus. Now she knew why she had flung herself into his arms at Pucallpa and unashamedly begged for his embrace just now. She was in love! She adored him. She wanted nothing more than to dedicate her life to him. He had torn the last shreds of independence from her with the release of his passion. Nothing mattered now except her love for Ian Morrison. Fever bordering on delirium raged inside her.

But he wasn't hers to love. He belonged to someone else—a someone, who, by her presence at the very moment of Carol's fall, had driven a knife into her happiness. Did Ian love Juanita? That she didn't know, but he called her his honey—the word itself stuck in Carol's throat— and that was enough. From now on she was condemned to watch her hostess and her lover progress through endearments to embraces to caresses—to his ultimate capture when they walked down the aisle of the cathedral together.

Her own deep love for Ian was doomed to remain forever hopeless, never to be returned. What was more, even the respect that she had so painstakingly built up in him was now dashed into smithereens, all because her guilt at the moment of discovery had made her run away, an action that he interpreted as a deliberate game with his emotions. It was now too late for explanations. She would never live it down.

Somehow she got her clothes off and crawled between the sheets. Head buried in the pillows, her slender frame racked by unquenchable sobs, she lay there until sleep claimed her from complete exhaustion.

The sun was already high in the sky when she woke to a gentle knocking on her door. "Who is it?" she called nervously.

"Teresa, la criada," came the answer.

Carol slid back the bolt, and the maid came in with her breakfast on a tray.

"Surely Señorita Muñoz didn't tell you to bring this?" she asked. She could hardly imagine Juanita being thoughtful toward her this morning.

"No, the señorita still sleeps," smiled Teresa. "But always on Sunday morning, I bring the *desayuno* to the bed."

"That's very nice," said Carol. "Is Señor Muñoz up yet?"

"Yes, the señor goes to church in a short while." Teresa shut the door gently behind her.

Carol remembered that she had half-promised Ricardo that she would go out with him today. It was the last thing she wanted to do now—in fact she didn't even want to meet Ricardo, whether or not Juanita had told him what she had seen in the garden. She would have to give some explanation for disappearing from his table at the banquet.

Vaguely she realized she had to make some plans. Life must go on in spite of her heartbreak.

She arranged the pillows comfortably behind her back and ate her breakfast. The stimulant effect of the strong, black coffee restored a degree of rationality. Her first decision was that she could no longer stay on at the villa, even if she wasn't asked to leave. Should she fly back to Albany on the next plane? No, that would be cowardly. And also unfair to Ian. Whatever he might think of her as a person, he needed her to complete his immunization program. She couldn't let him down.

So she would find a little apartment of her own in Iquitos and continue working until her job was done, suppressing her feelings for her employer with an iron will. That much decided, she dressed to go for a walk before Juanita got up, or Ian either. She needed to clear her mind before facing either of them.

There were no signs of life in the house when she slipped out through the front door. Her footsteps led her along the waterfront, deserted and silent without the usual weekday bustle.

As she walked she forced her brain to think along practical lines. Whenever she found her thoughts drifting to Ian, to his handsome graying temples, or to the crinkles around his eyes when he smiled, or, worse, to the touch of his sensitive hand, she bit her lip to keep her self-control. Then she would drag her errant thoughts back to how to make a dignified exit from the villa and how to set about finding an apartment on a Sunday. She was determined that the break would be immediate and quick. She never wanted to see Ian and Juanita together again—not as long as she lived.

Mooning along the foreshore, she came at length to the jetty where Antonio kept his motorboat. In her mind's eye she pictured the scene at seven thirty tomorrow morning when she would have to climb into the boat alongside Ian for the journey to the camp. She'd have to steel herself for the ride beside the man she loved more than anything in the world, and who now despised her for something she hadn't committed.

Antonio's boat wasn't tied up to the jetty. But standing near its usual place, peering upstream, was a young girl in a neat school uniform. She had the dark, flat features of a Yagua Indian, although her straight black hair was plaited at the back, and the commonly vacant expression of the Indians was missing. This girl had bright, shining eyes and a look of lively interest in all around her.

Of course, thought Carol, that must be Jutai's daughter,

Chicua, waiting for her Sunday visit to her father at the camp.

Without realizing she was doing it for the vicarious pleasure of talking to someone who knew Ian well, Carol strolled up the jetty to speak to the girl. Her opening words had already formed by the time she saw something that made her heart leap. Some of Ian's words and deeds took on a new, undreamed-of-meaning, falling together like pieces of a jigsaw puzzle. For the girl was wearing, on top of her navy-blue tunic, the necklace of semiprecious stones that Ian had clearly said he was going to give to his "honey"!

Barely controlling the excitement in her voice, Carol said to the girl, "Hello, you're Chicua, aren't you?"

Defensively, the little Indian replied, "My real name's Maria Luisa, but my daddy calls me Chicua, yes. How did you know?"

"Who else calls you Chicua besides your daddy?"

"Ian does—but he's a good friend."

"I work with Ian," said Carol. "I know your daddy, too. I'm a nurse, and my name's Carol."

"Carolina!" Chicua dropped her defenses on hearing Carol's name. "I know about you. Ian told me. He says you're a very good nurse. He says you're very pretty, too. He's right, you are pretty."

"Thank you," Carol replied, pleased that Ian had given a good report on her, though what did it matter now? "Tell me, Chicua, where did you get that necklace you're wearing?"

Chicua fingered the string of stones around her neck. "Oh, this. Ian gave it to me last week when he came to visit me at school. I'm not supposed to wear it with my uniform, but I took it to Mass in my pocket this morning, and put it on after. I love it so much, and as I'm going to see Ian today . . ."

"Ian's up at the camp?" asked Carol in surprise.

"Yes. He doesn't usually go there on Sundays, but he left a message at the school for me that he had gone up with Antonio this morning. He's coming back for me at eleven. What time is it now?"

Carol looked at her watch. "Nearly eleven. Ian's coming back here?" She wasn't ready to meet him again yet, in spite of the unbelievably good news that it was Chicua he meant when he talked about his honey, not Juanita at all.

"No, Antonio's coming back," said Chicua as though Carol was stupid. "Ian's up at the camp with my daddy for the day."

Carol cast her mind back to the innumerable times Ian had referred to his "honey," and Carol had mistakenly thought it was Juanita. At Manaus he had said he wanted to get back to Iquitos to see her, in Pucallpa he had said he missed her, in the boat he had said he was going to buy her a present. Every time he had used the word, Carol had felt a twinge of jealousy for Juanita—and now she had found out that it was little Chicua he was talking about all the time!

"Chicua," she asked, "does Ian often come to see you at school?"

"Oh yes. Most evenings, as soon as he arrives in Iquitos, before he goes home. The lady he lives with doesn't like him going out later, and she won't let me see me on Sundays either—until today."

"Has Ian told you anything about the lady he lives with? Has he said anything about . . . about marrying her, for instance?"

Chicua looked puzzled. "He hasn't said anything like that. I didn't think he liked her much, but had to live with her because of his job or something. Anyway, he's going to marry *me* when I grow up to be a big doctor like him. But I haven't told him yet . . ." Her face suddenly clouded. "You won't tell him, will you? I want it to be a surprise."

Carol laughed, "No, I won't tell him. I promise. Chicua, he doesn't ever talk about the other lady as his honey, does he?"

"No, of course not. *I'm* his honey. That means we're going to get married one day. I told you."

Carol's brain was spinning with the implications of what Chicua had said. It sounded as though Ian wasn't enamored of Juanita at all in the way that Carol had assumed.

Come to think of it, she had never seen him making any tender gesture toward her, or making any loving remark—it always seemed to be Juanita who had her arm around *him* and so on. Perhaps for his part, it was merely a friendship of convenience. If so, his heart was free, and she, Carol, was free to try and win him for herself!

The thought made her want to skip in the air. New hope flooded through her—she and Ian, it was a possibility after all! Of course Juanita wanted him, too, and she was formidable opposition, slowly breaking him down during cozy evenings at the villa, but Carol had no obligation now to adopt a hands-off policy. She need have no feelings of guilt when he took her in his arms . . . if only she had known this last night, that kiss might have lasted forever . . .

Carol's joyous conclusion, and the supreme fantasy that a repetition of that kiss conjured up, was interrupted by the arrival of Antonio in the motorboat, down from the camp to pick up Chicua.

"Carolina," Chicua was pulling at her sleeve, "wake up. Here's Antonio. Why don't you come up to the camp too? We could all have fun together. Ian would love to see you—he's told me how much he likes you, and I like you, too. Only the other day he was telling me how you had been away working together in the jungle and how great you had been. He said he wished you didn't have to be working all the time when you were with him—how he would love to have fun with you, too. He said he didn't want you to go away . . . ever."

Carol stared at her, "Ian told you *that*?"

"Honestly he did. If I didn't know that doctors never marry their nurses, I would be afraid he might marry you before I grew up."

"Did he also tell you that doctors never marry their nurses?"

"Yes, that's right. Or they shouldn't anyway. It doesn't work out, he said, a wife working for her husband. But he said it will be all right for me to marry a doctor, because we'd be equal. Come on, Carolina, come and get in the boat. We'll go and see my daddy and Ian."

Carol could hardly resist the temptation, especially now . . . now that she knew what Ian felt about her. But that was last week; surely he didn't feel that way about her any more. He might have been on the verge of falling in love himself—heavenly thought!—if so, it would have made his horror all the worse when he thought she had been merely playing with him . . . No wonder he had been so angry. His love will have turned to hatred now. She would have to try and explain it all to him, but this wouldn't be the time for a reconciliation, not with Jutai and Chicua there. A better opportunity would come later, perhaps tomorrow.

"I'm sorry, Chicua," said Carol. "I really would love to come with you, but I have other things to do today. We'll meet again soon."

Waving the little girl good-bye, and resisting the temptation to send Ian her love, she retraced her steps to the Muñoz villa. With luck, Juanita had kept to herself what she had seen, and wouldn't even mention it to Carol, not wanting to show her hand. In that case Carol wouldn't have to move, and everything could go on as before. Her lucky discovery that Ian was far from being engaged to Juanita, and that his affections might be leaning instead toward Carol herself—at least until her calamitous mistake last night—changed everything and filled her with buoyant hope.

Brimming with confidence, she walked into the villa. The living room was empty, so she passed through onto the terrace. There she found Juanita in her diminutive bikini, soaking up the sun on one of the garden couches. Giant sunglasses hid her eyes, but her mouth turned down in a disagreeable expression. Carol almost felt sorry for her; it must have been a shock to come upon the man you were making a play for kissing another girl.

"Good morning, Juanita," she said brightly. "Enjoying a nice lazy Sunday morning? I hear Ian's gone up to the camp."

"Yes," growled Juanita. "To get away from you, no doubt. I didn't discourage him. Sit down—I want to talk to you."

Well, if she wants to have it out, she can, thought Carol.

I don't care. She perched herself on the edge of the parapet so that Juanita would have to look upward to talk to her. "What do you want to talk about, the weather?"

"You can cut out the smart stuff right now. You know I saw your disgusting performance with Ian last night."

"Of course. But it wasn't a bit disgusting to me until I saw you watching us. That's why I ran away."

"Exactly. You must have felt very guilty. But Ian doesn't think that was why you ran away, does he?" Juanita took a sip from her glass of fruit juice and looked at Carol quizzically from under perfectly plucked eyebrows.

"Not unless you told him."

"Why should I tell him? I heard what he shouted at you. And I much prefer him to go on thinking that you're toying with him like a cheap . . ."

Carol bit her lip. "Before you start insulting me, Juanita, you should know that I've discovered this morning that I have as much right to his love as you have."

"Love? You think that Ian could ever love *you*? Don't be silly!"

"I have hopes that in time . . . when I've straightened him out about why I ran away. I wish I'd known then what I know now—I wouldn't have cared whether you were watching or not."

"What is it that you think you discovered this morning?"

"That Ricardo's story that you two are unofficially engaged is nonsense. I bet he hasn't even told you he loves you, let alone asked you to marry him."

Juanita threw out a mocking laugh. "So what? It's only a matter of days till Ian proposes. I have a lot more to offer him than you have."

"I might be able to make him change his mind."

"I'm seeing to it that you won't have the chance." Her voice had a ring of triumph. Carol wondered what this scheming woman had up her sleeve now.

"If you mean that you want me to move out of here, I'd already decided that if you were going to be unpleasant about last night, I'd go. But that won't stop me seeing Ian. I'll take a little apartment in Iquitos . . ."

"And prepare a little love-nest to lure him into? You think I would stand for that?"

"You can't stop me."

Juanita let out an exasperated sigh. "I don't think you understand your position, Nurse Baxter. I originally thought of sending you straight back to the United States . . ."

"Me?" Carol bristled. "You can't *send* me anywhere. I'm employed by Ian and . . ."

Juanita held up a languid hand to cut Carol short. "Just a minute, young lady. Let me finish. I decided that it would be best for you to continue working here. Without you, Ian's return to America—therefore mine—would be delayed, and that I don't want. So I've arranged for you to move in this afternoon with Marilyn and Pedro Roldan."

"What reason did you give? That I was queering your pitch with the man you hoped to snare?"

"No. I said that Ricardo's attentions were making it a little difficult for you here in the house. You will catch the supply boat to the camp every morning and go straight to Marilyn's when you come back in the evening. And under no circumstances will you go on any overnight trips with Ian again."

Carol found Juanita's instructions almost humorous. "And I suppose I'm not allowed to speak to him either?" she asked with biting sarcasm in her tone.

"That, unfortunately, I can't prevent. But you know Ian—he will refuse to discuss anything at all personal while he's working, and that's the only time you'll see him."

"You do regard me as a dangerous adversary, don't you?" That realization was the only pleasant thing about this ridiculous conversation.

"Not especially. But through your work you have certain advantages that I lack. And I don't intend to take any chances on losing Ian to some silly infatuated nurse who . . ."

"It's not infatuation! I love him . . . more than anything in the world . . . more than you do, I'm sure. And I intend to give him the chance to love me in return. You can't dictate to me!"

"But that's where you're wrong," said Juanita icily. "I can. You will do exactly as I say. You will keep Ian strictly at arm's length from now on. At least you will if you are as much in love with him as you think you are."

An uneasy falter crept into Carol's voice as she asked, "What do you mean? What will happen if I don't?"

"I wondered when you were going to ask that. You are obviously not aware of the influence I have with the authorities in this country."

"I know your uncle is the minister of health . . ."

"So Ian told you. In that case he probably also told you that it's very difficult for foreigners to get medical licenses in Peru. Ricardo and I arranged it through Uncle Mañuel for Ian to be allowed to work here. I can just as easily have his license revoked at any time."

"What would that mean?"

"That he would have to cease all work with his beloved Indians. He would have to go back to America, unable to finish the medical study he is doing on them—the study that will give him an international reputation. His most important life's work would be ruined. Now surely you wouldn't want to be responsible for that."

"He'd be disappointed, I can see that," said Carol thoughtfully. "But he's young; he could always go elsewhere to do his research . . ."

"That's not all I could arrange. With Ian gone I would see that that precocious little Yagua girl was expelled from her school and sent back to the bush where she belongs. If the loss of his study didn't break Ian's heart, stopping his grandiose plans for that girl certainly would."

"You can't!" Carol cried from her perch on the parapet. "I agree it would upset Ian terribly, but it would also deprive little Chicua and all that her success in school represents to the Indians—a chance for recognition at last . . . It would be a wicked thing . . ."

"Who cares about recognition for the Indians?" Juanita shrugged her bare shoulders. "All I care about is seeing that some little upstart of a nurse doesn't interfere with my marriage plans."

Carol was silent for a moment, thinking over Juanita's ultimatum. "But if you did these awful things to Ian, he would never marry you."

"That's perfectly true. But what a price you would have made him pay—and the girl pay, too—for the chance to try and win him for yourself! You might not even be successful, and he would have had to suffer just the same. You'd do that to the man you love?"

"You said you considered sending me home to the States. Would you have done that through your 'influence' in high places too?"

"Absolutely. The minister of immigration is a close friend. I could have had you out of the country this morning."

"Why didn't you? In spite of the delay to Ian's work, you would have got rid of me altogether and the threat that you seem to think I am to you?"

"Ian would have been furious at the disruption to his immunization program and would have asked awkward questions. I didn't want you to become any kind of martyr in his eyes."

Tears of rage and frustration welled up in Carol's eyes. "You devil!" she muttered. "You unspeakable heartless devil! Do you think I'm going to leave a good man like Ian defenseless against your conniving tactics? I'm going to tell him everything!"

"You won't, you know," said Juanita coolly. "Because if you do, he will lose his study, his reputation, and his little Chicua. You wouldn't do that to him, I'm sure."

"Then I'll bide my time, doing as you say, and wait until we're both back in New York. I don't believe he'll marry you before then."

"You'd be surprised. Your little performance last night was a big help to me. He became very . . . friendly . . . later in the evening."

Carol sat still, her breast heaving with indignation. What a sacrifice she was being called upon to make! She had to give up her one and only chance to win the man

114

she loved in order to save him from losing the two things most precious to him in the world—his imminent reputation as a famous physician and the little girl he had adopted as his protégée. The burden of the choice was almost unbearable!

"You've no choice, have you?" smiled Juanita, reading her thoughts. "Now you'd better pack your things and get on over to Marilyn's before Ricardo comes home."

"Ricardo won't let me leave this house," Carol said, grasping at straws. "He . . . he likes me."

"He did until I told him about the way you enticed Ian into that kiss last night. Now he wants you as far away from Ian as possible. He'll probably call you at Marilyn's—he hasn't altogether given up on you. By the way, you're welcome to Ricardo as a consolation prize."

Carol came as close then to spitting at someone as she ever had. But instead she walked off the terrace, head high and footsteps sure.

Two hours later, suitcase in hand, Carol was knocking on the door of the Roldans' pleasant suburban house. A manservant let her in, obviously expecting her, and gave her a note left for her by Marilyn. "Welcome!" it read. "Not as posh as the Muñozes', but I hope you'll be comfortable. At least you'll be safe from unwanted clutches! Sorry not to be here, but have an all-day invitation to the country. Pedro away till next week. The servants will feed you tonight, and I'll see you in the morning if I'm up before you go to work. Marilyn."

Carol mechanically unpacked and put everything away. The only time an involuntary shudder passed through her body was when she was handling her blue silk dress.

Although her mind was behaving as if she were in a dream, her outward composure was restored. The world kept on turning, heedless of the emptiness she felt inside. Nobody cared, not a soul anywhere, about the sacrifice she had to make. Ian would care, if he knew the whole truth—in fact he would probably explode—but who was to tell him? Not Carol, because if she did, the whole ghastly power of Juanita's vengeance would be unleashed upon him, and she would herself have betrayed him. No threat, even the certainty that she would now lose him, would make her betray her love for him. Her mind was made up.

Her only other thought was whether Juanita's threats had all been bluff. Did she really have the influence she said she had? Her uncle was the minister of health and handed out licenses, Ian had confirmed that, but would he do Juanita's bidding without question? Would the local authorities send bright little Chicua back to the bush if Juanita said so? Would the immigration people kick her, Carol, out of Peru at a moment's notice? Only one person she knew could answer these questions—Juanita's brother, Ricardo.

That was why, when Ricardo called her during the afternoon, she was polite to him. Surprisingly, he made no direct reference to the reason for her dismissal from the villa, but simply said he agreed that "it was for the best." He apologized for having let his attention be distracted during the banquet by the old bore who had collared him; he hadn't realized that Carol had had a headache and wanted to leave. Headache? So that was the story that Juanita had told him—she hadn't told him about the kiss at all. Juanita was a liar as well as a schemer—perhaps Juanita was lying about her "influence" as well.

It wasn't hard to wangle out of Ricardo an invitation to go to dinner with him at a little *típico* restaurant in the city. It had a *mariachi* band which played quite well, he said, and the food was as good as anywhere on the Amazon. He would pick her up at eight and promised to bring her home early, so that she would be full of energy for work tomorrow.

Ricardo was already waiting for her when Carol came downstairs ready to go out. She had no enthusiasm for an evening in his company, and had made no particular effort over her appearance. An ordinary little dress, her hair drawn back severely into a bun in the way she usually wore it on the hospital ward, sensible shoes, and little make-up—that was the way she felt like dressing tonight.

Carol's sole purpose was to pry information out of Ricardo. She had little doubt that he would be more than happy to talk about his important relatives in the government. He would probably think Carol was asking questions in order to determine his eligibility as a future husband. That couldn't be helped; let Ricardo think what he liked about her interest in him.

The restaurant *was* charming. Red checkered tablecloths and candles, a lively combo, which played "La Cucaracha" and other Mexican tunes that Carol liked, and waiters in colorful costumes. How she would have loved an evening here with Ian . . . !

"The *empanadas* are the specialty," announced Ricardo after he had sat her with her back to the wall so that she could watch the band and the dancing. "They're fried pastry shells filled with ground veal. I think you'll like them."

"That sounds fine, thank you," said Carol, trying not to sound bored.

"And what about some wine? Red or white?"

"Anything, thank you," she replied, "I really don't mind." She herself didn't feel like drinking, but some wine might loosen Ricardo's tongue. For that reason she decided to postpone her cross-questioning until after the meal. With his wits dulled, Ricardo would be less likely to become suspicious. Carol had no idea how much Juanita had told him about her plan to drive a wedge between Ian and herself. He might even be party to it for all Carol knew. She would have to tread cautiously because she was on dangerous ground. No report of her inquiries must get back to Juanita.

Ricardo had scraped the last morsel of a creamy dessert off his plate and was wiping his mouth with relish before Carol led off with her first innocent question. He had drunk more than his share of the bottle of wine, and his guard should be down by now.

"Tell me more about your family," she said. "I think you said some of them were well known in Peru."

Ricardo's long, rambling answer fell on deaf ears, anxious though Carol was to pick up any snippets which might help her. For he had no sooner started talking than the restaurant door opened and in came Ian and Juanita.

From where he sat, Ricardo had no view of them, but

117

Carol could watch them closely without appearing not to be listening to him. They stood at the door, looking around—Carol couldn't tell whether they saw her or not, but neither of them made any sign of recognition—then Ian, dressed in elegant sports clothes and looking more handsome than ever, casually slipped his arm round Juanita's shoulders and squeezed her to him. She looked up at his face with patent adoration before he let her go to lead the way to a vacant table.

Carol experienced a horrible sinking feeling in her stomach and felt the blood drain from her face. This was the first time she had seen Ian initiate such a gesture or exhibit any tenderness toward Juanita at all. It utterly dashed the hope she still nurtured that she might still have a place in his heart when the misunderstanding had been cleared up, if ever it was. She had lost him now for good.

In awful fascination Carol watched Juanita put her handbag on the table and immediately lead Ian to the dance floor. They slipped easily into each other's arms, Juanita nestled her head against Ian's shoulder, and his chin came softly to rest against her forehead. . . .

Carol could stand no more. "Please take me home, Ricardo," she pleaded. "I . . . I'm not feeling well. I must go home right now."

"You *are* looking a bit pale," said Ricardo, interrupting his own flow of words about his illustrious ancestors. "I'm so sorry, my little one. It must be all that awful work you do. I wish you'd let me put an end to it once and for all. . . ."

Carol got up and hurried to the door without another glance at the dance floor. In the car she sat huddled and silent except for one question. "Did you tell Ian you were taking me to that restaurant this evening?"

"Yes, as a matter of fact I did mention it. Why?"

"No reason," she whispered, feeling her body shrivel up inside.

Chapter 6

On leaden feet Carol made her way to the jetty for the start of another week's work. She had heard Marilyn come in while she was tossing on her bed last night, and she had left the house before her hostess had risen this morning. The sunlight filtering through the trees of the avenue she walked along and the happy cries of children on their way to school did nothing to alleviate her gloom. Normally a cheerful, optimistic person, this empty feeling of despair was foreign to her.

Although life seemed to hold nothing for her today, and although she dreaded meeting Ian on the boat, her sense of duty drew her to the camp. She had lost her love, but that didn't mean dozens, maybe hundreds, of Indians had to risk losing their lives from measles.

She was in the boat, waiting, when Ian arrived in his jeep. A strange numbness came over her as she watched him slam the car door and climb down to join her. He didn't speak to her—he didn't even look at her. He just sat there, a few feet away, staring out across the river as Antonio cast off and headed up toward the camp. From time to time on the way he would pass his hand across his mouth, deep in contemplation.

Ian was forced to acknowledge Carol's presence when the boat docked at the camp. They both made for the ladder at the same moment; then both hung back, waiting for the other to go first.

"After you," Ian said curtly, and Carol imagined she could feel the blade of his hatred piercing her back as he stood below, watching her climb.

Jutai was waiting at the top. "Good morning, nurse-lady," he beamed at her. "You see my Chicua yesterday? She tell me."

"Yes, I did," Carol smiled back. "And a delightful child she is. You have every right to be proud of her." And I have no right whatever, she thought to herself, to destroy all his dreams for his daughter in order to gratify my own selfish desires.

Ian's appearance beside them precluded further discussion. "This week," he said to Jutai without bothering with the formality of a greeting, "I want you to take Carol to the villages within an hour's paddling distance. Every single person in them has to be inoculated. She will leave with you as soon as she arrives on the boat, and you will bring her back to the camp by five o'clock each afternoon so that she can return to Iquitos with Antonio. Is that clear?"

"Yes, Señor Morrison," said Jutai, looking hurt by Ian's brusque manner. "And you? You will need me during the day? I can come back . . . ."

"I'll let you know. Not today anyway. I'll be working alone. And I'll be staying at the camp tonight. Probably every night in the future."

Carol's eyebrows rose. "You're not going back to . . . to the villa all week?"

Ian's cold stare shriveled her. "What business is that of yours, may I ask? Now get off to the village and start work. Pronto." He strode away across the platform and disappeared into Henry Todd's quarters.

Jutai watched him go, shaking his head sadly. "Señor Morrison not good today. Not good yesterday either—he seem, as you say, put out. He come to camp to see Chicua, but he not play games with her like other days!"

"That's too bad," said Carol noncommittally.

"Chicua excited because see you in Iquitos, but Señor Morrison he tell her shut up, not want talk about you. Chicua not like. Chicua cry."

"Oh, I'm terribly sorry," said Carol sympathetically. At that moment she came very near to running after Ian and pouring out the whole true story to him. She could so easily dispel his contempt for her, contempt that even reflected on his attitude to Chicua when the girl mentioned Carol's name. It was so unfair. Desperately she wanted to clean the slate, to make everybody including herself happy again when she held the power to do it, but yet she drew back, knowing that if Ian knew the truth, he would be bound to take some course of action that would bring the whole weight of Juanita's vengeance on him like an axe.

Better to let him suffer a bit now by keeping quiet— they would all soon forget her after she had left in a few short weeks—than be responsible for shattering their whole lives.

At the village Jutai rounded up each family in turn for their shots, and Carol worked steadily through them. They hardly spoke to each other, although once or twice she caught Jutai looking at her with a puzzled expression on his face, and when four o'clock came, they paddled back to the camp in silence. She left with Antonio without setting eyes on Ian again.

Pedro Roldan was still away, so Carol and Marilyn dined alone that night. Marilyn had cooked the meal herself as a treat for Carol—a typical hearty English dinner as a change from the spicy Peruvian dishes the native cooks always turned out.

"It's a treat for me, too," said Marilyn, when Carol congratulated her. "Pedro insists on South American food all the time so I never get to eat anything else. Actually it's just as well; a meal like this every night and my weight would take off like a rocket. I wish I could stay slim like you. All the good-looking men like tall, slim girls."

"That's a myth," replied Carol. "The short, well-padded ones win every time. Especially if they can afford to dress like princesses."

"Oh, you mean Juanita Muñoz. I used to think your boss was smitten with her, but I'm not so sure now."

"Why not?"

"Well, a couple of things," said Marilyn confidentially, warming to her theme. "For one thing I asked Pedro to find out why Ricardo is mad with Ian Morrison. Well it seems that Ian is being slower than Ricardo would like in popping the question, if you know what I mean. Everybody knows that Ricardo wants to get Juanita married off—she's burning up the family fortune on clothes as fast as he's losing it on the stock exchange—and until a couple of weeks ago it looked as though Ian was going to step into the breach. But the last time Ricardo tackled him on his intentions, to coin a phrase, apparently Ian stalled."

"What's the other reason you think Ian's lost interest?"

Marilyn pursed her lips coyly. "Well, my dear, *that* concerns you. Apart from seeing the way Ian was looking at you the other evening, I typed a report on you for him last Friday. I tell you, it was such a glowing account that I wondered . . ."

"Well, I did once have to feed him . . ." said Carol, brushing aside this outdated information, "but there won't be any more reports . . ."

The conversation was becoming too painful for Carol to continue, so soon after, Carol excused herself and went to bed.

A few evenings later, after a series of lonely days at the camp, during which Carol didn't see Ian at all, Marilyn had more to tell her about Dr. Morrison. Yesterday he had sent down for typing some notes on the medical study he was conducting on the Yaguas around Pucallpa.

"Of course I don't pretend to understand all this technical jargon," she said, "but it looked like something pretty important to me. He thinks he's onto something that will stop so many of their babies getting sick at about one year old. Some of them even die from a mysterious disease that may be to do with their diet—at that age they start eating meat that has been killed by some poison or something . . ."

"Yes, curare," said Carol. "I've seen one of the men do it."

"Well, this poison or whatever is bad for babies, according to Ian's idea, but not for adults. Anyway, he has to wait another three weeks before he can prove this thing—without the proof the study is useless—and he's afraid the floods will come before he can get out to a place called Pucallpa and other villages to make all his final tests."

The floods are not the only thing that'll stop him, thought Carol. If I as much as bat an eyelid at him and Juanita finds out, she'll wreck the whole study, and the babies will go on getting sick. Her resolve for self-control became even stronger. But if she was going to be able to endure her agony without cracking up, she had to share it with someone. Days of misery with the man she loved so near to her and yet so far—she couldn't stand it any longer.

"Marilyn," she said simply, "I'm in love with Ian, and I've . . . I've muffed the whole thing! He was kissing me and . . . and I ran away. I had to, I saw something that scared me—I can't tell you what it was. And now he thinks I've just been teasing him all along . . . and he hates me. Oh, Marilyn, what am I going to do?"

Confiding in Marilyn helped Carol sleep better that night. Marilyn had given her encouragement but not advice. Without Carol revealing why she couldn't approach Ian with an explanation for running away in the middle of his kiss, Marilyn said she was unable to help.

The level of the water lapping around the pilings on which the camp was built was noticeably higher next morning. The snows were melting in the mountains and the Amazon was rising.

Carol was surprised not to find Jutai waiting for her as usual. There was no sign of Ian either. She checked the medical office and all the store rooms, ending up in Henry Todd's bedroom. Knocking softly, she entered. She hadn't seen the old man for several days and was shocked by his appearance. He was lying on his bunk in a pair of pajamas, looking haggard and blue around the mouth.

"Come in, Carol," Henry smiled at her weakly. "How have you been?" He seemed to be having difficulty getting his breath.

"Hello, Henry," she said, coming up and taking his bony hand. "I've been fine, but what about you? I'm sorry you've been sick."

"It's this stupid heart of mine playing up again. Ian found I had fibrillation—irregular heart beats—the other day, but since he put me on digitalis, I felt much better . . . until an hour or so ago. Then this dizzy spell came on—I can't think what it is."

"Where's Ian now? I'll call him."

"He went off early this morning with Jutai . . . to collect material for his study. They'll be back this evening. I'll be all right till then."

Instinctively Carol felt the old man's pulse. It was weak and very slow, but regular. Thinking back to her days in the hospital cardiac unit, she took his blood pressure and listened to his heart.

"I forgot we had another doctor here," Henry quipped. "You're a very efficient young lady."

"You ought to be in the hospital, Henry," said Carol seriously. "I think you've developed a heart block as a result of the digitalis. It happens sometimes."

"I'm not going to a hospital," he said flatly. "With Ian and you to look after me, what more could I want? How do you treat this heart block thing?"

"Well, the doctors I used to work with stopped the digitalis and gave the patient quinidine. But I'm not a doctor. I've never done it without a doctor's orders."

"I'll trust you . . . Carol," Henry panted. His color was definitely worsening.

Her brain working calmly, Carol faced her dilemma. In a hospital she would be fired for changing a doctor's orders without his permission, but she knew what should be done—she was confident of that—and by this evening, if Henry's heart block went untreated, he would definitely be much worse. She had to do what she could. . . .

"I'll be back in a minute," she told Henry, and went to the medical office to look for some quinidine. She found a vial of it without much trouble, and armed with a sterile syringe, returned to Henry's bedside. Coolly she rolled up his sleeve and put on the tourniquet as she had done a hundred times before . . . but under a physician's direction.

The drug flowed into her patient's vein. She folded his elbow over a cotton-wool swab and lifted him into more of a sitting position. Then she stood there, feeling his pulse, waiting for the effect . . . Doubt began to creep over her as she watched him, still fighting for breath, his eyes closed. Had she done the wrong thing? Perhaps it wasn't heart block after all. In the hospital the doctor would have taken an electrocardiogram to confirm the diagnosis before treating it with quinidine. What would Ian have done without having the equipment for such a test? Would he have gone ahead as she had, or wouldn't he have taken the chance?

Half an hour later, Henry's color began to improve as his heart resumed a more normal beat. His pulse became stronger and his breathing easier. He opened his eyes. "Thank you, Carol, that feels ever so much better. You're a good nurse. Ian should give you a promotion."

"That's not what I need from him," she replied.

"Rather what I thought," smiled the old man, "but don't fret, my girl, Ian is not a man to be rushed. You should be glad about that."

"Glad? Why?" She hadn't realized that Henry had been so perceptive as to guess her feelings toward Ian, but as he had, there was no point in denying them.

"Well, he'd be married to the Muñoz girl by now if he'd been one to respond to pressure, from all I hear."

How had Henry heard anything, stuck away by himself up here? she wondered.

Carol left Henry asleep, propped up against his pillows, breathing well, and his face a healthy pink color again. The quinidine had undoubtedly done its work. . . . She had dealt satisfactorily with the patient—if only she could deal as well with the doctor!

The village where Carol had spent the last few days inoculating the Indians was not far away, up a small tributary of the main creek. She had paddled up there with Jutai each morning and knew the way perfectly. The route twisted and turned a certain amount, but there were clear landmarks and no serious obstructions.

She lowered herself into the smallest of the canoes that belonged to the camp and set off with firm strokes. The rise in the water level had obscured a few of the familiar logs along the way, and the creek was wider than it had been yesterday, but she had no trouble finding the village, and was soon at work injecting serum into the docile inhabitants.

Before her lunch break, great drops of water started plopping through the dense foliage overhead onto the ground beside her. She moved under cover of a thatched hut and continued her work. Coping with Henry had delayed her start this morning, and she wanted to make up for lost time. At four o'clock she calculated that if she kept going for another hour, she would be able to complete the program for that village and not have to return the next day. If Ian were annoyed with her for overstepping her position by treating Henry, he at least would have nothing to complain about as far as her regular duties were concerned.

Soon after five she packed away her equipment and started her journey back to the camp. The rain was coming down in almost solid sheets by now. It soaked through her safari suit and dripped steadily from the brim of her topee, but she was warm from the paddling and didn't care. Visibility was the only problem. That and the three or four inches the water had risen since she had come that way this morning. At a large dead tree she recalled that she had to turn left, and then keep her eyes open for a weird collection of roots sticking out of the water, which marked the place for a right turn.

The dead tree was there all right, but it seemed a lot farther than it ought to have been before she came to the roots. They didn't look quite right either, but she assumed that that was because they were more submerged now. She turned right and kept on going through the pelting rain. Nothing seemed familiar anymore. Insignificant streams through the undergrowth had grown to become considerable waterways. Hesitatingly she took one that her sense of direction told her was right, but it petered out in a tangle of undergrowth.

She backtracked now, searching for the roots or the tree, but could find neither. Her watch said half past six, and darkness was beginning to close in on her before she admitted to herself that she was hopelessly lost.

The jungle no longer frightened her; since the trip to Pucallpa she felt quite at home among the giant trees, the dangling liana, and the strident calls of birds and monkeys. But she had never been out in the dark before, she had never been out in such a downpour before, and she had never been alone and lost before.

Even so, she didn't lose her head. The camp couldn't be more than half a mile away, and there was no point in exhausting herself by paddling aimlessly. She would find a dry place to rest and wait for someone to come and find her.

But who would come? Suppose Ian and Jutai had got caught in the storm, too, and had decided not to return to the camp until tomorrow. Henry wouldn't even know where she had gone, and anyway, he was too weak to think of raising the alarm—he probably imagined she was on her way back to Iquitos by now. Only Antonio would know; he would still be waiting in the boat for his passenger. Antonio would come looking for her . . . she hoped.

Pinning her faith in Antonio, she hauled her canoe onto a piece of high ground, actually an island with ever-widening stretches of muddy water on all sides of it, and created some shelter by propping it against the trunk of a huge, gnarled tree in an upside-down position. She filled in the empty gaps with branches and dead leaves. In this makeshift tent she sat down to wait for help to arrive.

Half an hour later it was quite dark. The stumps and bushes around her became no more than ghostly shadows. She could just make out the water line, creeping inch by inch toward her. Still the rain poured down relentlessly. But Carol was made of strong stuff; she refused to let herself be claimed by fear.

Her island was diminishing in size rapidly now. Carol retreated as the waters encroached. She dismantled her tent and carried the canoe to the highest point; the rain once more beat mercilessly upon her. But even there the squelching beneath her feet told her that her refuge would soon become a swamp. And after that it would sink below the surface of the swirling torrent and become an unrecognizable part of the whole engulfing flood.

She bit her lip to ward off panic, as mysterious shapes glided by. They were only logs after all, set afloat by the rising tide. She moved farther back yet and took up a position on the roots of a tree, crouching with her back to its massive trunk. Somehow, she now decided, she must do something to attract attention, to do something that would guide Antonio to her. With all landmarks obliterated, there was no hope of him finding her otherwise.

A fire would never burn in this deluge; she would have to make some sort of noise. So she laid her canoe upside down across two of the sprawling tentacles at her feet and started pounding the bottom with a heavy log in imitation of the native drums. The sound reverberated well but was hardly a match for the noise of a million raindrops.

Realizing that she might have to keep this up for some time, she developed a routine. Rhythmical banging on the canoe followed by a call through cupped hands, "Antonio! Help!" repeated again and again.

For over an hour there was no response. The water lapped all around her now. But still she kept up her desperate call for help. The long gray form of another log drifted toward her and stopped a few feet away. Then, strangely, it began to rise out of the water and poised motionless on a mud bank, its form taking shape as she focused upon it. In the dimness two pinpoints of red directed themselves straight at her.

Terror finally overtook her as she realized that this huge, gaunt mass was no harmless log. It was a crocodile, jaws open wide for the inevitable snap that would take her leg off . . .

Carol screamed at the top of her voice, much louder than her cries for help had been. As if in response, a flashlight beam swung in her direction from across the water not far away. The light began to bounce up and down. She yelled encouragement at it; the crocodile didn't move.

It soon became apparent that the flashlight was being held by someone paddling a canoe. It swung back and forth with each stroke. When the boat came close, the crocodile closed its vicious teeth and slid silently away.

Carol brushed sodden strands of hair away from her face in a gesture of intense relief.

"I'm here!" she shouted, furiously waving her arms, "I'm here! Can you see me? I'm marooned at the base of this tree."

The beam from the flashlight bobbed uncertainly and slowly toward her, but at last, following Carol's frantic calls, the canoe grounded on the mud a few yards from her feet.

"I still can't see you," said Ian's voice, "but I could have heard that scream a mile away. What was up? Are you hurt or anything? Can you walk?"

"I saw . . . a . . . crocodile," she gasped, "but it's gone now. Another minute, and I swear it would have gone for me."

"But you're all right?"

"Yes," she replied shakily, "I'm all right. Just awfully wet, that's all."

"You're not the only one," Ian said grumpily. He swung the flashlight round until he caught her in its beam. "Ah, there you are. Come and get in the boat and let's go home. You're going to have some explaining to do, I can tell you. You'd better have a darned good excuse for being out alone in this weather."

Carol started picking her way toward the outline of Ian's canoe. "You've got no right to be angry with me!" she sputtered at him, a surge of annoyance quickly replacing her sense of relief. "But thank you for rescuing me just the same."

He made no acknowledgment of her thanks, but just sat there slumped on the back seat, holding the light. She came up beside him, her boots sinking into the mud, hoping for a hand to help her in. But no hand stretched out—he seemed to have no wish to touch her. Clumsily she tried to climb into the seat in front of him, but her foot slipped, and she fell in a heap onto his lap. His arms closed around her, and in that instant everything became all right again. She lay there, reveling in his closeness and the comfort of his arms, her heart thumping wildly. Her problem evaporated—all that mattered now was that they were together, welded and inseparable.

But it didn't last long. "Come on, up you get!" he said. "We'll leave your canoe here for now. Let's get back to camp."

Reluctantly Carol struggled to a sitting position. Picking up the spare paddle, she pushed the canoe off the mud, and they were on their way. She and her love, alone together at last. How she longed to tear down the invisible barrier between them, to right the wrongs, to pour out the truth, and to give herself another chance for his affection! But the awful burden of her responsibility for Ian's own reputation, for Chicua's future, and for the Indian babies' health, weighed heavily upon her. She said nothing.

"What were you doing out of the camp alone?" he asked sternly.

"Just my job," she called over her shoulder. "What did you expect me to do? You left me no instructions, so I went to the village."

"I did so!" he replied indignantly. "Didn't Henry Todd tell you? No, he probably forgot as a result of his attack."

Here it comes, thought Carol, at this moment of all moments, the dressing-down for counteracting his medical orders. She paddled on stolidly, waiting for his angry voice to continue.

After a while, he spoke again, but his tone was soft, almost reverent. "Carol, where on earth did you learn your cardiology? Henry told me you diagnosed heart block and treated him with quinidine. There's no doubt at all that you were right. It was a terrific piece of work . . . without even an electrocardiogram. You may well have saved his life."

"Blessed words of praise!" she said. "I thought you'd be mad."

"Far from it. I was most impressed. In fact, I felt compelled to come out in this downpour to rescue a nurse as good as you when I'd seen what you did for Henry."

"No other reason?" Carol asked wistfully.

"Not particularly," Ian replied, his tone hardening, "although I have to admit you're a remarkable girl. It must have taken a good deal of courage, too . . . But then you *are* pretty sure of yourself, aren't you? So sure that you think you can fool around with guys . . ."

"Ian, please!" she begged. "Please don't go on!"

They paddled on in silence after that, Ian guiding the way until they came to the camp.

"Jutai went off in the other canoe to look for you," said Ian, consulting his watch. "I told him to come back by nine if he hadn't found you, so he'll be back soon. You have one friend in this camp, Carol; Jutai wanted to continue the search all night if necessary."

"While you'd have quit and gone to bed?" asked Carol poignantly.

"Well, I don't know," Ian replied, avoiding her eyes. "Fortunately the situation didn't arise. Now you better get some dry clothes on and go back down to Iquitos. Antonio's still waiting."

"I haven't got anything to change into. My other clothes are all at Marilyn's."

"Oh . . ." he hesitated. "Well, in that case, you'll have to borrow something of mine. Come with me."

Carol followed him to the room he used as a bedroom. It was as bare and stark as a trapper's cabin in Canada. A hammock stretched between two posts, a suitcase of jumbled clothes, a desk covered with books and papers, a pile of opera records, a photograph of an elderly couple, presumably his parents. At least there's no memento of Juanita, thought Carol.

"Here," he said, rummaging in the suitcase and producing a shirt, a pair of jeans, a sweater, and some sandals. "They'll be much too big for you, but they'll have to do. I don't keep a lady's wardrobe up here, I'm afraid."

"I'm glad I qualify as a lady in your eyes," Carol remarked with a wry smile.

He looked at her for a moment, almost tenderly, but then quickly looked away. "Always ready with a wisecrack, aren't you?" He thrust the pile of clothes at her and told her to hurry up and change. "And, by the way," he added, "you don't have to come in tomorrow. You can have the day off . . . as long as you don't . . ."

"Don't what? Don't go out with Ricardo?"

"I didn't say that. Anyway nothing I can say to you stops you from doing what you want, so I've given up bothering." He stalked out of the room, leaving Carol to take off her soggy suit and boots and put on his absurdly oversized outfit. Though it bagged all over her body, she felt deliciously snug and intimate in it.

She ran in to see Henry before she left. "How are you feeling?" she asked. He was certainly looking much improved.

"Good," he assured her, "thanks to you. Ian is very pleased with you, you know. He can't understand how a nurse knew what to do."

"Ian doesn't have a very good opinion of nurses," she replied. "Especially this one."

"He'll change his mind in time. He's confused right now, but he'll get over that, don't worry."

"Thanks, Henry." She pressed his hand warmly. "I won't be in tomorrow, but I'll see you on Monday morning."

"Fine. I'll be here. I'm not going anywhere just yet. Ian and Jutai are leaving for a longer trip on Monday, so I'll be glad to have you around just in case . . ."

She left Henry then and went across to the motorboat. Antonio was more surly than ever at having been kept waiting for so long, and Carol made no attempt at conversation.

Snuggled up in Ian's sweater against the cool night breeze in the open boat, she relived those precious few seconds when he had held her in his arms. In spite of his rough talk, he had been glad she was safe—of that Carol was certain. But whether it was because he felt a degree of responsibility for her safety, or for more personal reasons, it was impossible to tell.

Pedro had come home for the weekend, and he and Marilyn were finishing a late dinner when Carol walked in and joined them.

"You look like a waif of about fourteen in those clothes," laughed Marilyn, after Carol had related her adventure. "Well, I'm glad he rescued you anyway."

"I'm glad it was him, too," said Carol. "Though I would have been almost as pleased to see anyone at all at that particular moment."

"Oh Carol," said Pedro, "Ricardo has called you twice this evening. He wants to take you to the army zoo tomorrow afternoon."

"To the what?"

"The local army unit has a zoo here," Pedro explained. "It's made up of all the animals and birds they have captured during their maneuvers in the jungle. It's interesting; you'll like it."

Carol pondered for a minute. Ricardo had phoned three times already that week, inquiring after her health and inviting her back to the *típico* restaurant for a better evening than last time. She had begged off—she had no wish to go dancing with an amorous Ricardo. But the zoo in the daytime would be less of a strain, and might satisfy him for a while. She did owe him something for walking out on him twice in a row.

"I'm off to bed now," she told Pedro. "If he calls again, tell him I'll go to the zoo with him tomorrow. Thanks a lot."

She went upstairs for a hot bath and the rest she needed in her comfortable bed.

"Ricardo's coming for you at two o'clock," Pedro informed her the next morning.

"Oh, that's when Ian's coming over with some typing for me," exclaimed Marilyn. "What fun! Perhaps they'll have a duel on our front lawn. Whose second will you be, Pedro?"

"Neither. I'm keeping out of that row. Though I do sympathize with Ricardo somewhat. Ian does seem to be playing it a bit fast and loose with Juanita, so I can see him being upset. What I don't understand is why Ian is angry with Ricardo."

"Ian told me that Ricardo had betrayed a trust," Carol put in, "but I can't think what that would be."

"Betrayed a trust?" Marilyn repeated. "*I've* an idea what that might be. I'll tell you later." She winked at Carol in a way that signified that she had kept Carol's secret from her husband—knowing Marilyn, Carol appreciated the self-control that must have required.

Ricardo arrived promptly at two o'clock, dressed in his usual blue suit and highly polished shoes. Carol had changed into a simple, but attractive, white linen dress and had let her hair hang loosely. After a week in the jungle, she felt like making the best of herself, even if it was only for Ricardo.

Walking with her to his car, Ricardo grew bolder and slipped a hand around her waist. "Ah *carísima*," he said with an expansive gesture of the other hand. "Today I will give you the world!"

Carol couldn't help being amused at his ridiculous attempts to impress her. She looked up at his dark face with its villainous mustache and burst into laughter. He looked back and they laughed together—until, simultaneously, they caught sight of Ian watching them from the open door of his jeep. He was standing, a clutch of papers in his hand, glaring as if murder were on his mind.

Ricardo, his arm now tighter around her waist, hurried her into his own car. Leaping in as fast as his bulk would allow, he started the engine and drove off, glancing in the rear mirror to see if he was being followed.

Only when they were several blocks away did Ricardo relax. "That man!" he muttered through his teeth. "One of these days I will do him an injury, a serious injury. Every day I think of you, my sweet Carol, toiling under his iron fist, and every day I swear to myself that I will release you from your jail."

"It's not a jail, Ricardo," Carol protested. "I could leave any time I want . . ."

"Then why not, why not?" He suddenly stopped the car and took her hand in his. "Carol, the other evening at the banquet, I did not get the chance to explain myself fully. You must think, 'That Ricardo, that South American, he is just flirting with me,' but I assure you it is not so. As soon as my sister leaves, I intend to bring my own lovely bride into La Casa del Corona . . ."

"She will be a lucky girl," said Carol evasively. "And I know you're sincere, Ricardo. But I'm just not thinking about marriage right now. Only last month I broke off an engagement . . ."

"Oh, what a fool the man must be to have let you go!" he expostulated. "Would that I might have such a chance! All right, my dearest, I can see that your poor heart must have time to mend. But I will be waiting, waiting with growing impatience, I may say. You must promise to let me know when I may dare to speak to you of it again."

"I will, I promise you," Carol said kindly, withdrawing her hand from under his.

He started the car again, and they drove to the edge of town before turning into an imposing driveway past a sentry who saluted him smartly.

The car came to rest at the entrance to the zoo. Ricardo led Carol through, pointing out the parrots with their brilliant plumage, sleek leopards pacing their cages, and a fat black tapir, like a pig with a long snout. Carol thought how Henry Todd, the naturalist, would be distressed to see the animals in such confinement, but refrained from any more remarks that might offend her guide.

Soon it started to rain, and Ricardo took her to the officers' mess for refreshments. He sat her in a deep leather chair in the huge, mahogany-paneled room decorated with swords and photographs, all of stiffly posed groups of uniformed men. A steward brought *churros,* little deep-fried cakes, and cups of cocoa, the traditional Sunday afternoon snack.

The commanding officer came to join them, resplendent in his gold braid and medals. "My friend!" he greeted Ricardo with a comrade's hug. "How glad I am to see that you are again to be found in the company of charming ladies!" He pressed Carol's knuckles to his lips in obvious admiration.

"Gently, friend," Ricardo chided him. "This one is like one of your little birds outside. She keeps trying to escape from her cage."

"But you will tame her in time," replied the colonel. "Even my restless leopards now permit me to stroke them."

"A cage is no way to bring a woman to submission,"

said Carol. "She always has to go of her own free choice, *preferring* life under the will of the man she loves to a life of freedom."

On the way back to the Roldans' house, Ricardo tried to persuade Carol to spend the evening with him. But she steadfastly refused, and, dodging his attempt to kiss her, ran through the rain from his car to the shelter of the house.

That evening at dinner, Marilyn seemed to be excited over something. Carol felt sure that it had some connection with Ian's visit during the afternoon, but no opportunity arose for her to speak to Marilyn alone. Eventually she went to bed.

Refreshed after her day off, Carol arrived at the camp by nine in Antonio's boat. Threatening clouds hung overhead although the rain had temporarily stopped; the level of the water had risen another foot since Saturday. She was surprised that Ian hadn't been on the boat too. Surely he had spent the night at Juanita's after visiting Marilyn.

Her first thought was for Henry Todd, and she was on her way to his room when Ian called her. He was standing with Jutai alongside the three-man canoe, already loaded with gear.

"How come you haven't left on your trip?" she asked. "Henry said you were going away again today."

Ian smiled at her—the first time in what seemed like an age—his deep gray eyes pierced her in that way that always made her feel a little faint. "We were waiting for *you*," he said. "We're going back to Pucallpa for a couple of days. I know how you like Pucallpa. Hurry up and change—you're coming with us."

Carol gulped. How she longed to go! If there had been any way she could have gone without Juanita finding out, she would have. But Juanita often phoned Marilyn in the evenings on some pretext or other, but no doubt mainly to check that Carol was safely in her cell.

"I . . . I can't," she stammered. "My jungle suit's still wet."

"No, it isn't," he replied. "I dried it in the kitchen when I got back from Iquitos yesterday afternoon. I decided then to take you with me today."

"You . . . you did? Why, what happened in Iquitos besides your seeing me with . . .?"

A frown creased his brow. "It was nothing to do with that. I just decided that you weren't quite what I thought you were."

"I wasn't? You mean you . . .?"

"Yes," he was smiling again. "I realized that I had made a bad mistake about you. Come on, hurry up and change. We've a long way to go!"

Carol knew she couldn't go with him, but she desperately wanted to hear him say that he now understood why she had fled from his embrace—that they could start again as friends. Marilyn must have told him of Carol's love. A blush came over her at the thought that he knew . . . Marilyn shouldn't have done it, but yet . . . bless Marilyn for it. His smile was worth the embarrassment.

"A mistake?" she repeated.

"Yes. I thought you were rather an incompetent little public health nurse who didn't know anything except how to immunize people. After what you did to Henry, I changed my mind. Now I know you can be a lot more help to me than that. I need you for my study on the Yagua babies. That's what we're going to do at Pucallpa."

Was he fooling? she wondered, or was this really why he wanted her now? Regardless of his personal feelings, was he being nice to her simply so as to obtain her help with his study, the study on which time was running out? The answer didn't make any difference to his request. She still couldn't go with him for fear of Juanita's reprisals.

"I'm glad your regard for me has improved," she said, "but I'm still not going to Pucallpa with you."

"You mean you're afraid that the witch doctor there will put a hex on you if you go back." He took a few paces toward her and placed both hands gently on her shoulders. "I'll protect you from any hexes. Come on . . . please!"

His touch sent her pulse racing. She felt herself on the verge of weakening. Only the certain knowledge that she would destroy him if she did saved her from taking the fatal step.

"No . . . no, I won't!" She shook herself free from his hands. "My contract is to do immunizations, not to do medical research. If that's what you're going to do, you can do it on your own."

"Carol, you must believe me," he pleaded. "There's been a dreadful misunderstanding between us . . ."

"You can say that again," she retorted, forcing a sharp tone into her voice. "I'm not going with you, and that's flat! For one thing, Henry's not well enough for us both to leave him."

"So that's it. Well, I appreciate your concern for Henry, but I can assure you as his doctor that he'll be fine as long as he stays in bed, and he's promised me he will. Now go and change, Carol, please! You'll be helping to save a number of other lives if you come now."

Carol couldn't bear Ian's entreaties any longer. She knew she would break if she listened to another word. She turned and ran to hide behind the corner of one of the buildings. Peeking out, she saw him shrug his shoulders in resignation and lower himself wearily into the canoe. She stayed there, staring into space, long after he had gone, thankful that her love had given her the strength to resist. . . .

In time she pulled herself together and went to see Henry. "You're looking a lot better today," she said, putting on her cheerful nurse's manner.

"Feeling better, too," replied the old man. "I heard the call of the Great Kiskadee outside just now. That's a bird that's not found in these parts. I'm going to take my binoculars and look for him."

"You're going to do nothing of the sort," said Carol sternly. "Ian left strict orders that you're to stay in bed. You're to stay in bed tomorrow, too. Or Ian will be furious when he gets back. You wouldn't want that, would you?"

"Not when his temper has taken a turn for the better," agreed Henry. "Something must have happened in Iquitos yesterday—he came back in a better mood than he's been in all week."

"That's probably Juanita's doing," she said.

"I don't think he saw her," said Henry. "I don't think he's as involved with Juanita as you think."

People kept telling her that Ian liked her—Chicua, Marilyn, and now Henry. But when had he shown it? One kiss, a spur of the moment thing inspired by the moonlight and the champagne—that was the only hint he had ever given that he found her attractive.

No, unquestionably his heart still lay in Juanita's ample bosom, whatever dear old Henry's opinion might be. Ian hadn't even admitted that his mistake about her had been on a personal level—he had changed his mind about her professional ability.

When Carol returned to the Roldans' house that evening, she found a note from Marilyn that she and Pedro had gone out and wouldn't be home till late. It was disappointing. She had been impatient all day to ask Marilyn what had transpired between her and Ian the previous afternoon.

Next morning Carol had little will to go to the camp. She was not going to risk another canoe trip by herself to continue the immunization program in a distant village, so she would have to undertake the boring job of cleaning the medical office.

But she was galvanized into action as soon as she got out of the boat. Henry Todd, fully dressed, was lying on the platform, moaning and clutching his chest.

Carol rushed over to him. "Henry! Henry, what is it? Why are you out of bed?"

"I . . . got a sighting on the Great Kiskadee . . . and . . . this pain in my chest . . ." His face was pallid, his eyes glazed.

She laid him down gently on the wooden boards, a cushion from one of the chairs under his head. "Now don't move. I'm coming back."

She ran into the office and came out with some instruments. His heart beat was weak but steady; his blood pressure low but not too bad. She gave him an injection of Demerol.

Gradually his limbs relaxed as the pain diminished.

"Thank you, thank you, Carol . . . That's much better. I . . . I'm sorry to give you this trouble."

"You know you shouldn't have got up. You promised me . . ."

"I know, but . . . What is it, Carol? What have I got?"

She looked at him thoughtfully, her fingers still on his pulse. "You've had a coronary, Henry—a heart attack. Luckily not a very serious one. I've seen enough of them to know. But it's the second in a few days—your attack of heart block was almost certainly due to a coronary, too, even though you didn't have any pain. You could get a third one any time, and that might well be . . . be fatal, Henry."

"Fatal?" He stared at her with watery eyes. "I'm not in any hurry to die . . . not yet. I must record that Great Kiskadee before I go. It's important. The Smithsonian would want to know about it. What can you do to stop the third one, Carol?"

"*I* can't do anything. But a heart surgeon could. There's a new operation for patients like you. The little hospital in Iquitos doesn't have the facilities, but in Lima they do. I'm taking you to Lima on the next plane, Henry. And I don't want any argument!"

Henry nodded his acquiescence. "I'm in your hands, Carol. Just get me to Lima and back here well again." He was still straining his tired eyes into the trees above him when Carol returned with Antonio and a workable stretcher made out of Ian's hammock. They strapped Henry into it and lowered him into the motorboat.

"Get as near as you can to the airport," Carol instructed Antonio. "And go full speed."

Less than an hour later, Henry was in a wheelchair in the lounge of Iquitos Airport. Carol was in a phone booth talking to Marilyn.

"I need some money," she was saying. "Urgently. Enough for two tickets to Lima and a hotel for me for a few days."

"My dear, I don't have that much in my account. And Pedro's gone off again. Why don't you ask Ricardo? He'd lend it to you like a shot."

Carol hesitated. "I can't bear the idea of being obligated to Ricardo. But I guess I'll have to. There's no one else . . ."

She hung up and dialed the number of the Muñoz villa. Fortunately Ricardo answered; she wouldn't have liked to talk to Juanita. Carol explained the situation in as few words as possible. Ricardo promised to come to the airport right away with as much money as she would need.

"Thank you very much," she said. "I knew you wouldn't let me down."

"It is an opportunity I wouldn't miss," he replied, and hung up.

Ricardo bustled into the airport a short while later, quite the businessman in a black Homburg hat and a raincoat over his arm. After a brief greeting to Henry, he took Carol's arm and led her to the ticket counter.

"When does the next plane leave for Lima?" he asked the clerk.

"At twelve o'clock, señor. In exactly one hour."

"Good," He turned to Carol. "That will give you time to take a taxi to the Roldans' house and collect some clothes. Bring your prettiest things. Lima is a well-dressed city. I'll stay here with Henry."

"You're being very kind, Ricardo," said Carol sincerely.

He gave her a stiff bow. "It is my pleasure, *carísima*." Then he turned to the ticket clerk. "Three return tickets to Lima on the twelve o'clock plane."

Carol stared at him for a moment. "Why three tickets? I only need two. For Henry and myself."

Ricardo smiled, a slow, self-satisfied smile. "I of course am accompanying you. My suitcase is in the car outside, already packed."

Chapter 7

From her window seat in the steeply climbing plane Carol looked down on the green velvet carpet of the jungle and thought of Ian somewhere in there, bravely facing the hardships and the dangers in order to pursue the work he loved. How she hoped he would approve of her decision to take Henry to Lima! She had been right last time, but was she straining her limited knowledge of heart disease too far in suggesting that he was a candidate for surgery? Was she taking too much of a risk in moving him so far right after his attack?

Her patient slept quietly in the seat next to her. His frail chest labored with each respiration, but his color was promisingly pinker than the ashen pallor of two hours ago. Beyond him, across the aisle, Ricardo was engrossed in his airline lunch.

As Ricardo had pointed out when she had protested against his coming along, she had no alternative but to accept his terms. She had less than a hundred dollars in her purse, whereas he had plenty of money for the trip. After taking Henry to the hospital, he had told her, he would take her to stay at the house of his Uncle Manuel, the minister of health. He would also show her the sights of Lima during her visit. Those were his conditions. Meekly she had agreed, although she would have preferred the freedom of a small hotel to the mansion he said his uncle lived in.

The jungle ended in foothills; then the formidable jagged peaks of the Andes Mountains passed below them. Soon after that they began their descent onto the coastal desert. Lima first took shape as a huge, sprawling oasis; as they flew closer, it became a core of high-rise buildings with never-ending suburbs and, beyond it, the blue of the Pacific Ocean. They landed in a modern steel and glass airport.

Within minutes she and Ricardo were in a taxi following the ambulance to the City Hospital. There he waited patiently while Carol arranged Henry's admission and described his illness to the doctor in charge of cardiology. Henry himself gripped her hand in pathetic gratitude when she left.

At last she emerged from the vast hospital complex, her mission completed. She climbed into the taxi beside Ricardo. Then and only then did she allow herself to relax for the first time that day. Compliant, she made no effort to turn away when Ricardo planted a tentative, bristly kiss on her cheek. If he went no further than that, it was a small price to pay for Henry's health.

Bursting with pride, Ricardo ushered her into the library of his uncle's house. "Uncle, I would like you to meet Miss Baxter. I have brought her to Lima from Iquitos on what I hope will be the first of many visits. Carol, this is my uncle Don Manuel Muñoz."

"Well, Ricardo, this is a surprise." The portly, energetic-looking man rose from behind his large, leather-covered desk and perfunctorily kissed Carol's hand. *"Encantado,"* he greeted her with twinkling eyes. "So you will be coming to Lima often? Are you taking employment here?"

Before Carol had a chance to reply, Ricardo's chest swelled and he said, "On the next occasion, I trust Miss Baxter will be here to purchase her wedding gown and to try on the gold band that I will be buying for her."

"Oh, Ricardo!" exclaimed Carol, aghast. "You have no right to say things like that! Señor Muñoz, I am no more than a friend of your nephew's."

"Friendship can mean many things. But as any kind of friend of Ricardo's, you are most welcome in my house. Your name is Carol? Please call me by my first name also." Don Manuel smiled benevolently.

"You haven't told me, Carol, are you a working girl?"

"Yes, I'm a nurse," she replied. "I'm on a temporary assignment in the jungle outside Iquitos, immunizing the Indians against measles."

Manuel's face lit up. "Congratulations, my dear. As the minister of health for this country, my major concern is to improve the plight of our Indian population. Their future is the future of Peru. One day their blood will be inextricably mixed with the Spanish blood of families like mine. I wish Ricardo would set the trend by marrying an Indian girl." He gave Carol an obvious wink while Ricardo turned away in disgust, muttering into his handkerchief.

While Carol and Manuel were sipping sherry that evening, waiting for Ricardo to join them, Manuel again brought up the subject of Carol's work. Although she had quickly changed into a sweater and clean pants at Marilyn's house before catching the plane, she had felt that a simple dress would be more appropriate for dinner with a minister of state and was looking demurely attractive.

"Your life in the jungle has not caused you to lose your feminine tastes," Manuel commented appreciatively. "How I admire you North American women! One minute you can be covered in grease fixing a car and the next looking as though you had never worked a day in your life. I wish more of our girls were the same."

"It's the men," said Carol. "Peruvians don't like women to work."

"Not *their* women, I agree. Does the man in your life mind, Carol?"

"There isn't one," she laughed. "But I work for a Dr. Morrison, Manuel, and he's doing marvelous things. I'm proud to be associated with him. Do you know, he's . . ."

"Morrison?" said Manuel, interested. "But that's the name of the American doctor Ricardo was talking to me about earlier this evening. Ricardo thinks I should revoke his license to practice when it comes up for renewal this week. He says this man is conducting all sorts of unorthodox experiments on Indian babies."

Carol nearly dropped her sherry glass. "You'll excuse me," she said icily, gaining control of herself, "but that's a complete lie. I work with Ian Morrison, and I should know what he's doing better than Ricardo does. Actually he's studying the effects of curare-poisoned meat in Indian babies' diets. He's onto a big discovery . . ."

"Is he now?" said Manuel. "I've been waiting for some physician to do research into that. It sounds like a very valuable contribution."

"It is," Carol went on. "Please let him keep his license, Manuel. The real reason why Ricardo wants Ian's license taken away is that he wants him to leave Iquitos. He thinks Ian's philandering with his sister Juanita and . . ."

"Juanita!" exclaimed Manuel with a hoarse laugh. "That tough little piece of goods! Nobody could ever philander with Juanita. Or if they are, she deserves it, the gold digger!"

The revelation of Manuel's opinion of Juanita was music to Carol's ears. Another lie exposed. So Juanita had no "influence" whatever with the minister of health! That meant that her threat to put a stop to Ian's study was merely bluff. But of course it didn't mean that she couldn't get Chicua expelled from school, and it didn't mean that she couldn't persuade the immigration authorities to force Carol out of the country. Perhaps this was a chance to find out.

"I'm so glad you don't listen to Juanita when making decisions, Manuel. I really don't think you should listen to Ricardo either."

"I won't, I promise you. I'm glad we had this little chat."

"Juanita says she is friendly with the minister of immigration," Carol pushed on boldly. "Is that true?"

Manuel shook his head sadly. "Alas, it is. The poor man is completely in her clutches. He worships the ground she walks on. And at his age . . . he should know better. But there's nothing I can do about that, unfortunately."

Ricardo came in to join them at that moment, and soon afterward the three of them went in to dinner. Carol was pleased that her host kept the discussion on generalities until bedtime.

Although she was very annoyed with Ricardo for trying to get Ian's license removed, Carol agreed to go shopping with him the next afternoon. It had been part of her bargain with him to let him escort her through the city. It would also be an opportunity to buy a new dress, the first since Christmas.

In the morning she went to see Henry Todd, timing her arrival at the hospital to coincide with the visiting hours. The doctor told her that they had agreed to open-heart surgery after performing a series of tests the previous day. In spite of his age, his general physical condition was good, and they had every hope of a successful outcome. She had acted intelligently in bringing him to Lima; a delay might have been too late.

The operation was scheduled for that afternoon, and Carol promised to come back later on, so as to be there when Henry came round from the anesthetic. If the doctors would give their permission—and it seemed likely, she being a nurse—she would stay with him all night.

"You're treating me like one of your family," said Henry with tears in his eyes. "When you're a lonely bachelor like me, that's a great comfort."

"I think of you all as my family," said Carol. "You, Jutai, Chicua, and Ian . . . especially Ian."

"Good luck to you on that score," Henry smiled, and she knew what he meant.

Until lunchtime Carol wandered through the streets of Lima, admiring the modern architecture as well as the old Colonial houses with projecting wooden balconies and carved outside beams. But her mind never strayed far from Ian and Juanita's threat. Now she knew that her rival didn't have the power to destroy the momentous work project he had set himself, Carol felt like throwing down the gauntlet and openly approaching Ian as soon as she got back to Iquitos. But, she asked herself sadly, if she did that, how would Ian himself react when the police ejected her from the country a few hours later? He certainly wouldn't follow her, leaving his precious work behind—why should he? She was no more to him than a good nurse. No, if she did that, it would be tantamount to leaving the field open to Juanita, and Juanita could weave a whole bewitching web in three weeks. She would be

Mrs. Ian Morrison before Carol ever had the chance to see him again.

On the shopping expedition Ricardo insisted on behaving as though they were lovers on the brink of an engagement. Carol's deprecating remarks bordered on frank rudeness, but he was undeterred, taking her hand and slipping an arm around her waist at the slightest excuse. He must have a hide like a rhinoceros not to realize that his oversolicitous attentions were unwelcome.

He took her into a shop which sold silver jewelry and other antiques. "Peruvian silver is known the world over," he said. "All upper-class women in Lima have a pair of silver earrings, so that is the first thing I will buy for you." He selected a pair of heavy loops and handed them to her.

"But I'm not a Peruvian woman," she said, examining the trinkets. "And I have no intention of becoming one. Besides, you need pierced ears to wear these, and my ears aren't pierced."

"In that case you will have them pierced—immediately."

"No, Ricardo, I won't," she said firmly. "I wish you would stop telling me what I will do and what I won't do."

"Now, my *bonita*, do not be angry with me. In time you will come to follow my suggestions."

Carol avoided further argument by going to look at some exquisite antique woodcuts in another part of the shop. There she chanced upon a beautifully executed picture of a large bird sitting on a branch. The label underneath read "Great Kiskadee 1869."

"You can buy me this if you like," she said to Ricardo, who was hovering over her shoulder.

"If that is your desire," he agreed with a sigh. When he had paid over a considerable sum of money for the woodcut, they left the shop. Carol was delighted with her find. It would be just the thing to inspire Henry through his convalescence.

In a dress shop on the Avenida República she also found exactly what she wanted: an imported caftan made of soft dark green muslin, light as a feather. With the hood pulled half over her shining auburn hair and the

147

cream tasseled cord tied around her waist, it gave her an air of casual elegance, like a fashion plate. She bought a pair of high-heeled sandals to match.

After an early supper that evening, she went to the hospital to see Henry. Carol propped up the woodcut where Henry would see it when he awoke and settled herself in a chair for her vigil. A doctor in a white coat came to do his evening rounds. In halting English he explained that Henry's postoperative condition was good considering his age. She was immensely relieved at the news; Henry would pull through—her dramatic flight from Iquitos would be justified.

Soon after midnight he stirred and opened his eyes. He smiled at her through the plastic of his oxygen tent and nodded faintly in recognition when she showed him the woodcut. Then he relapsed into sleep again, and Carol herself dozed off in her chair.

In the morning she helped one of the nurses with his bed and decided to stay for a few more hours, so as to be there when he regained full consciousness.

She was actually standing with her back to the door, looking out of the window at the hospital gardens below, half-daydreaming about a very similar garden away across the Andes—the one belonging to the *ayuntamiento* in Iquitos—when Ian came in.

"I see my nurse has done it again," he said gently.

She whipped round to face him, her heart giving a great leap.

"Ian!" she cried, "Oh, Ian, I'm so glad you've come!"

"I got the story from the cardiologist downstairs," he said. "There's no doubt you saved his life this time." With a practiced eye he ran through the notes clipped to the end of Henry's bed and watched the jiggling needle on the electrocardiographic monitor. For a moment he studied Henry's features, still in repose—then he walked slowly over to where Carol was standing, her face flushed with delight. He took her by both shoulders, smiling his crinkly smile, and the ground swayed beneath her feet as he placed a tender little kiss on her forehead.

"You astound me," he murmured, releasing her and

sinking into the chair. "How on earth did you have the presence of mind to bring him into Lima for surgery? No other nurse I know would have dreamed of taking that responsibility."

"Maybe I'm no ordinary nurse," she smiled mischievously, "but how did you know where to come?" she asked. "I see you're still in the clothes you went to Pucallpa in."

"Yes," he replied. "Pretty grubby for a smart hospital, aren't they? But Jutai and I didn't get back to the camp till late last night—my research into curare is going great, by the way; another two or three days in the bush, and I'll have all the data I need—anyway, Antonio told me you'd taken Henry to the airport, so I guessed the rest. I'll never underestimate you again, Carol."

"I'm glad of that. But what did you do then?"

"Well, I snatched a couple of hours' sleep at the camp and took the boat to the airport before dawn. I just made the first daily flight to Lima. That's how I'm here so early."

"So nobody in Iquitos knows you're here?" The tantalizing thought that Juanita would still think he was in Pucallpa had occurred to her. Carol could break the rules Juanita had imposed without any fear of her indiscretion being discovered. All she had to do was prevent Ricardo finding out they were together—better still, prevent him from finding out that Ian was in Lima at all—and she was as free as the wind to be seen anywhere with Ian, doing anything with Ian! In this huge city nobody would recognize them. Surely he would invite her out somewhere. . . .

"That's right," he was saying. "It's lucky I had enough money up at the camp for the airfare and everything. You must remind me to pay you back for all your expenses when we get home again."

Carol didn't answer. Somehow she didn't want to mention Ricardo's name at that moment. Time enough to explain that later.

"You know, Carol," Ian went on, looking again at Henry's peaceful, sleeping form. "You were quite right to refuse to come up to Pucallpa with us. Henry wasn't in any condition to be left alone without any medical help."

"This wouldn't have happened if he'd stayed in bed as you'd ordered him. I found him outside trying to get a sighting on some rare bird—this bird as a matter of fact." She showed Ian the woodcut. "He recognized the Great Kiskadee when he came round a few hours ago. I think it cheered him up."

"You bought this for him?" asked Ian in a way that fortunately didn't require an answer. "And you've been here with him all night? You really are a sweet, thoughtful girl—as well as everything else!"

Carol could hardly hold back the joy she felt at his words.

"I try . . ." she said modestly.

"I don't think so. I think it comes naturally to you. Anyway, as I was saying, you were right to stay with Henry. That *was* why you wouldn't come to Pucallpa, wasn't it?"

"Yes . . . yes, it was," she lied. What else could she say?

"I thought so. It's uncanny intuition you have—almost a sixth sense. At the time I thought it was because you couldn't stand any more of my company . . . particularly at Pucallpa again."

Carol smiled at the memory. "How was the waterfall? Did you sleep in the same hut?"

"Yes, I did. But I didn't sleep very well. Disturbing dreams kept waking me up."

"Dreams about a bad, bad girl by any chance?"

He grinned at her and hesitated for a long minute before answering. "Maybe. By the way, that reminds me. I had a talk with Marilyn that day I took my notes in to her for typing."

"Yes?" she said, her heart in her mouth. How much had Marilyn told him?

"It seems that I wasn't quite fair to you when you shoved me away from you that evening at the wedding banquet. Marilyn said you had some reason . . . that you'd seen something."

"Yes . . . yes, I did see something. It scared me. I'm sorry now. I wish . . ."

"What was it? The ghost of your ex-fiancé come to haunt you?"

"No, that wouldn't have put me off. It was . . . it was Juanita watching us. I suppose she didn't tell you."

Ian looked puzzled. "No, she didn't, as a matter of fact. That's surprising. She's a great one for getting all upset over little things like that."

Little things? thought Carol in dismay, is that all that kiss meant to him? Aloud she said, "I thought she'd be upset, and so I panicked. It was stupid of me."

"You certainly needn't have. Juanita has no strings on me. If I want to kiss a girl, I kiss a girl."

You say it as if you'd been raising your hat to me in the street or shaking my hand or something! thought Carol miserably. Did that kiss really mean so little to you?

Calming herself, she asked him, "You're not thinking of marrying Juanita then?"

He looked at her hard, unsmiling, his gaze seeming to pierce her inmost soul. "Well . . . yes, I suppose I have considered it."

"And what have you decided?"

"Nothing . . . yet. And anyway, it's not only my decision, you know. I doubt if she'd want to marry me."

"Oh, Ian! How could anybody . . . ? I mean, I'm certain Juanita's crazy about you. I've seen her looking at you in that way."

He got to his feet with a little sigh and came close to Carol again as she stood by the window. "Why are we talking about Juanita?" he said. "She's not here to watch us in Lima."

"I don't know," she replied in a small voice. "Let's not anymore." He laid his hands gently on her hips and smiled at her upturned face. The room started revolving at the thought that he was going to kiss her again, but he didn't. A bare hospital room with an unconscious patient in it at ten in the morning was hardly an appropriate place for the kind of kiss she longed for. He walked slowly away and said, with his back to her, "We could meet somewhere this evening if you like."

Problems rushed through her brain. What excuse could

she make to Ricardo? How could she get back late into Manuel's house? But she dismissed them all as irrelevant.

"Okay." She tried to make her voice sound casual. "Whatever you say."

He turned round to face her. "Good. But the first thing I must do is buy some clothes and check into a hotel. Where are *you* staying?"

The truth had to come out now. But it wouldn't matter any more. This evening could be the turning point in their relationship. On this evening she was pinning all her hopes.

"I'm not actually staying in a hotel," she said. "Ricardo took me to his Uncle Manuel's. I had to . . ."

"What!" Ian's face blanched with rage. "You mean you're with *him*? He's here in Lima? You came here *together*?"

"Ian, I didn't want to, I swear to you. But I had to borrow the money from Ricardo . . . And he insisted on coming . . ."

"You borrowed money from that. . . that rotter? Carol, how could you . . . ?" He was nearly screaming.

"What else could I do? I didn't have nearly enough . . ."

"You could have done anything, anything at all, rather than go to him of all people! You could have gone to *my* bank, you could have told the airline it was an emergency, you could have . . .

"It seemed the quickest thing to do . . ." she wailed. "Please understand . . ."

His tone of voice suddenly became cold steel. Between clenched teeth he spat out his accusation. "I don't believe a word of it, Carol. I think the two of you had a trip to Lima planned all along, and Henry's illness just provided a convenient excuse. You knew I was away in the jungle, and you decided to take advantage of it."

"Ian, listen . . ." she pleaded, but nothing would divert him.

"All right, you can have your Ricardo. You can be sure *I* won't interfere with your lovers' tryst in the big city."

And he slammed out of the door down the passage. The room became deathly silent. Distraught, Carol looked at

Henry. He had just opened his eyes again and was searching for her. Dutifully, she went over to the bed to comfort him.

It was nearly noon by the time she returned to Manuel's house. She had been up all night and had had no breakfast. All she wanted to do was to eat something and go to bed without talking to anybody.

But Ricardo wasn't going to allow her the peace she desired. He came and sat with her while she consumed the omelette and toast which the cook had prepared.

"Are you sure you stayed in the hospital all night?" he asked suspiciously.

"What else do you think I did?" she answered curtly.

"It seems strange to me. This man Todd isn't a relative of yours, so I can't see why you would give up your rest . . ."

She sighed and put down her fork. "Henry Todd happens to mean a lot to me, and I don't care if you don't understand. Anyway, I'm going up to bed right now for a long sleep."

Ricardo pulled a gold watch out of his vest pocket. "Not too long, I hope. You and I have a date tonight."

"A date? Since when?"

"Since I got two tickets for the sound and light show at the ruins of Quetzal. It starts at eight."

Carol's first reaction was to refuse to go.

"What is this show?" she asked cautiously.

"The ruins of Quetzal are what remains of a fourteenth-century country house built before the Inca conquest. The show consists of music and dancing to illustrate the life of an Inca princess. It will be your first lesson in Peruvian history."

Carol had no particular reason to want to learn Peruvian history but decided that the entertainment might be what she needed to help her over her distress. She agreed to be ready for an early dinner and to go with him to the ruins afterward. Ricardo apparently hadn't even considered the possibility of her refusing.

Carol did sleep that afternoon. But not without first fretting over the loss of precious time that was being

wasted, time when she and Ian could have been together . . .

By six she was downstairs again dressed in the same delicate little dress she had worn the first evening. She encountered Manuel in the library.

"Ah, come in, my dear," he said. "I hear Ricardo is taking you to Quetzal this evening. I hope you will enjoy the
show."

"I hope so, too. But I must admit Ricardo twisted my
arm."

"Carol, please forgive my interference, but do I sense
that my nephew is, shall I say, forcing himself upon you
more than you wish?"

"Well," Carol laughed, "he does rather think of himself
as irresistible, doesn't he?"

"And you are well able to resist him. Is that it?"

"He does have some nice qualities, Manuel, but . . ."

"But your heart belongs to someone else. Since you told
me there was no man in your life, it must be someone
who doesn't return your affection. I am sorry. It's an old
story, but still a sad one."

"If only Ricardo wasn't so persistent . . ." An idea
came to her. "Doesn't he have any other girlfriends in
Lima? Surely there must be somebody."

"There *is* a girl," said Manuel, dropping his voice. "In
my opinion she is very suited to Ricardo, good family,
steeped in tradition, and very fond of him. He used to
take her out before he got engaged to that woman in Iquitos . . ."

"The one who died?"

"That's right. I always hoped he'd go back to Francesca
after that. But he never has, perhaps because you came
along. Tell me, would you like me to try and arrange
something?"

"If it would take some of the heat off me," Carol
laughed. "I'll go to the ruins with him tonight, but after
that I'm afraid I'll have to start turning him down. He
only brought me here because of an emergency, you know.
Apart from anything else, it isn't fair to him for me to
keep dating him. He may start getting ideas . . ."

"That's very considerate of you. You can leave it to me, Carol. I will bring Francesca back into his life again. She would be delighted, I'm sure. And he . . . well, you never know."

Ricardo seemed tremendously excited by the prospect of going to Quetzal. He was jumpy and twittering in the taxi, although they were at least half an hour early. And when they had passed through the gate under the big banner *"Son y Luz,"* he led her quickly away from the open-air theater where the performance was to take place to a quiet grove of trees at the foot of an ancient stone pyramid. He appeared to have something planned; Carol became nervous.

"Mi carísima," he began, "the show you will see depicts the arrival of a Spanish nobleman at the castle of an Inca king to seek the hand of his daughter, a beautiful princess . . ."

"But I thought the Spanish conquistadores pillaged the country and seized the women, not wooed them. See, I do know some Peruvian history after all."

"Please don't interrupt. As I was saying, the princess at first refused the Spaniard's advances, but in time she came to love him, and eventually they were married and founders of our great nation."

"If you say so . . ."

"In the case of you and myself, the foreign princess has come to the home of the Spaniard, but otherwise the story is the same. This is the moment I have chosen, my dearest Carol, to ask you to accept this ring as a formal symbol of our betrothal."

He then pulled from his pocket a flashing ring of blood-red rubies and diamonds and advanced toward her, intent on placing it on her finger.

Carol was completely taken aback. Ricardo's well-rehearsed proposal would have been comic if it had not been, in his eyes, so deadly serious. She was unable to comprehend his blindness to the way she had been putting him off ever since they had met.

It was also curious that he had made no mention of love; it seemed that he didn't regard love as a necessary ingredient of marriage. His physical advances toward her had also lacked fire or imagination—for that she was grateful—but did he really think that she would accept his offer of marriage when she had never responded to the slightest degree to his half-hearted attempts to kiss her? Yet he was a man who was incapable of taking no for an answer. If she gave him a flat refusal now, the subsequent scene would last all evening. If she told him she loved someone else, he would pester her endlessly until she gave his name. No, the only thing to do right now was to stall.

"Oh, Ricardo," she said, putting on an act of breathless bewilderment. "You take me completely by surprise!"

"Surprises are one of the spices of life, my dearest," he beamed. "We will have many surprises in our years together, I feel sure. Here, now take the ring and wear it with pride."

"I can't, Ricardo, I just can't," she said. "I must have time to think about it. Please!"

He stood up straight from his position leaning over her. "I suppose that if you need time, I cannot deny it to you. Perhaps the ring will help you with your decision. If you will not wear it, you will at least keep it. I shall expect to hear from you soon. Come, we will now go to watch the *son y luz*. Perhaps the entertainment will inspire you."

To have escaped from this awkward situation, even if only temporarily, was as much as Carol could hope for. Gingerly she took the ring and put it in her purse—it must have been worth well over a thousand dollars—and let him take her stiffly by the arm and lead her to the auditorium.

The sound and light show was such an interesting presentation that it drove from Carol's mind the problems associated with the man beside her. As she watched the dancers act out a love story between an Incan princess and a Spanish nobleman, Carol found herself engulfed in another of those uncharacteristic fantasies in which she became the princess, and her lover Ian, not Ricardo. She saw herself proudly spurning his advances, leaping gracefully through the air, hiding behind the ancient stone pillars that dotted the stage, but finally succumbing to his persistent charms, prostrate and expectant. Ian, after bandishing his sword about her cowering form, stepped back and waited for her voluntary submission. Slowly, as if propelled by some supernatural force, she rose and moved toward him . . . Then, abandoning all semblance of control, she ran helter-skelter into the arms of his embrace. Carol felt herself trembling in the rapture of the moment.

The audience burst into frenzied applause. Then people started preparing to leave, and a voice behind Carol said, "It seemed to me you did enjoy it."

She and Ricardo turned round simultaneously. Carol looked into the smiling face of Manuel Muñoz, but Ricardo stared at the placid features of the girl beside him. "Francesca!" he gulped.

"So you two still recognize each other," said Manuel. "Francesca, this is Carol, a guest in my house. Ricardo has been acting as tourist guide this evening."

"What . . . what are you doing here?" Ricardo mumbled to Francesca. "I haven't seen you since . . . since . . ."

"Your uncle kindly invited me," Francesca spoke in a soft, well-modulated voice, obviously the product of strict training in the art of being ladylike. "It's nice to see you again, Ricardo. And a pleasure to meet *you,* too." She bowed her perfectly groomed head toward Carol.

"Come," said Manuel, reaching for his hat and standing up. "I know Carol is tired, as she was on an errand of mercy all last night, so I will take her home. Ricardo, it will of course be a pleasure for you to take Francesca. I'm sure you remember where she lives."

"Naturally, uncle," Ricardo replied in a low voice. "Come along, Francesca."

"Didn't you think I arranged that well?" Manuel chuckled as he showed Carol into his car. "I took a look at my nephew's tickets and bought seats right behind you. Francesca had quite given up on ever seeing him again."

"You were very kind to go to all that trouble, Manuel," said Carol with honest gratitude. "It certainly made things easier for me tonight. But I still have tomorrow to cope with."

Tomorrow, she thought, yes, tomorrow. Another day with Ian in town and Juanita still safely miles away. And unless I can arrange something, another day in which we won't even see each other. Maybe I should go and spend all day in the hospital. He's bound to go and visit Henry.

Carol ate a leisurely breakfast in bed next morning. While sipping her coffee she decided that the first thing she would do would be to seek out Ricardo—if he wasn't already lying in wait for her—and put an end to any misconception he might have that she was going to marry him. There was no point in prolonging the farce. She would give him his ring back and tell him straight.

But when she went downstairs, the ring in her hand, he was nowhere to be seen in any of the living rooms. The door of the library was closed, and she hesitated to disturb Manuel at his work, but she wanted to get the unpleasant ordeal over; Manuel would know where she could find Ricardo.

She knocked and heard the minister call "Come in!" When she opened the door he was sitting at his usual place behind the desk, and lounging comfortably in the chair opposite him was Ian.

"Ah, there you are, Carol," said Manuel, getting to his feet. "I don't need to introduce you to Dr. Morrison. I'm glad you've made an appearance at last—the doctor and I have long since finished our business, but I had the feeling he wasn't going to leave until he had seen you."

Ian stood up, a sheepish grin on his face. "Hello, Carol," he said. "I hear you've been putting in a good word for me. Don Manuel has just renewed my medical license. I appreciate it."

She remained by the door, the hand holding Ricardo's ring concealed behind her back. "You didn't expect me to let anyone get away with stories that you were conducting unorthodox experiments on babies, did you? It would reflect on me as your assistant."

Manuel coughed. "Yes, Ricardo does get some funny ideas at times. By the way, Carol, you may be interested to know that he's gone to the beach with Francesca. Dr.

Morrison seemed surprisingly interested in that small piece of information, too."

"Yes, I . . . er . . . think I owe you an apology, Carol," said Ian. "I put two and two together and made five. Don Manuel has straightened out a lot of things for me. It appears that the relationship between you and his nephew is much more one-sided than I thought."

"What would it matter to you if it wasn't?" In spite of Manuel's presence in the room, Carol desperately wanted to hear Ian answer that question. He usually flew into a temper whenever Ricardo's name was mentioned; in front of the uncle, he could hardly do that.

But Ian was evasive. "I don't have to tell you that, Carol."

Manuel moved round from behind his desk and laid a hand on Ian's shoulder. "So you're going back to your camp tomorrow. It's been a great pleasure to meet you. Keep up the good work."

"Yes, I must go back. The last few days of my study are the most important. I wouldn't have left at all if my old friend Henry Todd hadn't been having surgery in Lima."

"And if your nurse hadn't come to Lima with him, perhaps," said Manuel with a wink at Carol, which made her cringe with embarrassment.

Ian apparently missed the inference of Manuel's remark. "I phoned the hospital this morning, Carol. Henry's much better. Will you be going to see him during visiting hours this afternoon?"

"Yes, I'll go at five o'clock. Will you be there?"

"Of course. And I'll want to take you back with me tomorrow on the 10:00 A.M. plane." His tone had very suddenly become authoritative.

When Ian had gone Manuel turned to Carol and remarked, "If that's the gentleman who holds the key to your heart, I wouldn't have thought you had much to worry about. I've seldom seen a man behave in such a jealous manner."

"Jealous?" repeated Carol, as the implication slowly

dawned on her. "You think Ian is jealous of Ricardo . . . because of me?"

"Why not? He certainly has designs on you himself."

"Oh, I hope you're right. But he's never come out and said it. I thought he didn't like me seeing Ricardo because he hates him."

"That seems to be mutual."

Remembering that Juanita mustn't know that Ian was in Lima, Carol said, "Don't tell Ricardo that Ian was here, will you?"

"It might be wiser if they are enemies," Manuel agreed. "But I wonder why Morrison dislikes my nephew so much. He didn't know until just now that Ricardo was trying to get his license revoked."

"Ian once told me that Ricardo had betrayed a trust of some kind. Before that they were friends."

"Perhaps *you* had something to do with that," Manuel mused.

"Me?" said Carol. "Oh, no. It happened before I ever came on the scene. It couldn't possibly have anything to do with me."

She went up to her room and put Ricardo's ring back in her purse. If he came home from the beach before she left for the hospital, she would give it back to him then and immediately dive for the door before he could make a scene.

The thought of going to the hospital filled her with optimism. Not only would she find Henry much better, but she would see Ian again, a contrite, friendly Ian. Would he be friendly enough to ask her out when visiting hours closed at six o'clock? Juanita would never find out, so they still had the chance for one evening together before going back to Iquitos. Carol racked her brains for a method of insuring that he would ask her out. Suddenly it came to her, and she tore out of the house, counting the small amount of money she still had left after her purchases.

Not risking the price of a taxi, she hurried along the busy downtown street on which Manuel's opulent mansion was located, until she came to a major intersection. There ahead of her was the building she had noticed on her way to the Quetzal ruins last night. She had noticed it with morbid sadness then, but now it took on a new significance. The building was the Lima Opera House.

The opera playing tonight was Bizet's *Carmen,* and the performers were a good European company. It started at seven—that would give them time to dawdle over dinner afterward.

Carol didn't have enough cash for the best seats, but the ones she could afford were not bad, in the orchestra stalls about halfway back. Bubbling with excitement over her inspiration, she hurried back to the house. She wanted to leave plenty of time to dress before going off to the hospital.

There was no doubt about what she was going to wear—her new caftan and high heels. After a long, luxurious soak in the bathtub, she arranged her hair in the loose, rather slinky style that fitted her mood. Stuffing her lipgloss and eye shadow into her purse along with the opera tickets, she put Ricardo's ring on top, intending to return it to him on her way out of the house. But Manuel came out of the library to tell her that Ricardo had not yet come back from taking Francesca swimming.

"And where are you off to now?"

"I'm just going up to the hospital," she explained.

"And that's all?" he replied with a twinkle. "Do you always dress up so elegantly to go visiting the sick?"

"It's important to keep up the patient's morale," she said.

"And the doctor's," quipped Manuel, retiring behind his door.

Ian was already in Henry's room when Carol arrived. His approving look at her appearance said more than words could have. So far, so good, she thought to herself.

Henry was still very weak, but obviously improved. He was out of the oxygen tent, and the intravenous had been disconnected, although the electronic monitor was still recording his heart action. The woodcut of the Great Kiskadee was prominently displayed where he could see it, and an immense bouquet of flowers brought by Ian stood on his bedside table. His smiles were those of a man well on his way to recovery.

They stayed with Henry until a bell announced the end of visiting hours. Then they took the elevator down to the ground floor and walked together along a broad white-tiled corridor toward the main lobby. In a minute they would be outside and bound to go their separate ways—and Ian still hadn't said anything about going out.

In the lobby she stopped and opened her purse. "Does this interest you at all?" she said, handing him the tickets.

He looked at them carefully, "*Carmen*, eh? I suppose you know what this opera's about."

"A Spanish girl, I think, a pretty wild one."

"That's right. She works in a tobacco factory in Seville, and she has two men fall in love with her, an army officer and a bullfighter."

"Which one does *she* love?" asked Carol out of ignorance.

"That's the point of the story. Neither of them. She gets a kick out of playing one off against the other." He paused meaningfully.

"Oh," Carol began to think she had made a wrong choice of opera. It seemed to be opening old sores, for he was giving her a poignant look.

"It's a dangerous game, that. Carmen gets knifed in the end."

She turned away, feeling the color drain from her cheeks. "I didn't know. Now I'm not sure I want to see it."

He laughed and snuggled her against him, his movement restoring her mood but upsetting her equilibrium with its delicious spontaneity. "It's only a tale—an excuse for Bizet to write some super arias. The story isn't important. But you surely know the 'Toreador Song.' It's terrific!"

"Can you sing it?"

"You bet!" Totally uninhibited, Ian jumped onto a hospital trolley and bellowed "*To-re-ador! To-re-ador!*" to the amazement of the dozens of staff, patients, and visitors thronging the lobby.

Carol burst into joyous laughter. This was her old Ian!

He jumped down off the trolley before anybody had a chance to comment. Then he walked calmly over to a couple of nurses who had applauded his singing. He asked them in Spanish if they liked opera, and when they nodded he gave them the two tickets, telling them to enjoy themselves.

Carol was dumbfounded. Why had he done that? Was the story of *Carmen* really too close to home for him? Was it his way of refusing to go out with her?

She was on the point of taking flight from the humiliation when he took her arm and showed her two other tickets for tonight's performance of *Carmen,* which he had just produced from his wallet. "Better seats," he said. "I hope you don't mind."

Carol felt like collapsing with relief, but she merely smiled and said, "Why should I mind?"

"Then come for a drink and some *tapas* at my hotel while I change. You know, after what you said about opera in Manaus, I was finding difficulty screwing up the courage to ask you to come. I wasn't going to mention that I'd got tickets until I'd given you some wine."

"You *were* going to ask me out then?"

"That was going to take courage, too, after what happened a couple of nights ago. I'm really sorry, Carol . . ."

"Forget it. It's tonight that counts."

Ian had a rented car in the hospital car-park. He had picked it up at the airport when he arrived and was going to turn it in there tomorrow—he said it was easier than taking taxis all the time.

They climbed into the car and drove to the Hotel Pax, a small, but palatial Colonial-style hotel in the heart of the city. There he picked up the key for his suite and escorted her to the fifth floor.

"What a gorgeous place!" she said, examining the period furniture and heavy brocade drapes in his private lounge.

"It's a nice change after the camp," he admitted. "Make yourself at home while I bathe and change. Drinks will be up in a minute."

An enthusiastic rendering of the "Toreador Song" was

coming from the shower when a waiter arrived with champagne in an ice bucket and dainty little *tapas* of fried
shrimps, squid, and other delicacies. He popped the cork
off the bottle and discreetly withdrew before Ian came in
from the bedroom dripping with water and only a towel
around his waist. Carol started—the last time she had seen
him like that was when he had carried her from the waterfall. That seemed an age ago; she hadn't even realized
then that she loved him.

He poured her some champagne—it tasted as heady as
nectar there in his room with him—and took a glass for
himself to drink while he changed next door. "We'll have
dinner after the opera if you can last till then. Meanwhile,
stoke up on those *tapas*. They'll keep the hunger pains
away."

Presently he emerged, looking more handsome than ever
in a smart new light gray worsted suit, and took her off,
slightly giddy with champagne and her own joyousness, to
the opera house. The seats he had bought were the best in
the house—in the middle of the front row of the mezza-
nine. No wonder he had given her tickets away. She
thought of the two little nurses tucked away underneath
them in the stalls, enjoying a rare treat for girls on a Peruvian nurse's salary. How thoughtful of Ian to surprise
them!

The opera was spectacular. When not gasping at the
costumes or carried away by the music, she was absorbed
in the beauty of the sets. The singing enthralled her, especially the now-familiar song belted out by the toreador
from the table top in the Spanish inn. She and Ian exchanged knowing smiles.

"For someone who doesn't like opera," he whispered,
"You seem to be having a remarkably good time."

"I'm allowed to change my mind, aren't I?" she grinned.

Still humming tunes from the performance, they took
his car to a very exclusive restaurant on a terrace overlooking the Río Rimac, the river that runs through Lima.
Fairy lights hung from the trees above the white linen tablecloths and gleamed off the silver and glass. A single
rosebud stood in the middle of each table. An illuminated

fountain played to one side, just audible above the soft music coming from unseen speakers. It was just the setting for Carol's perfect evening.

A waiter in a long tail coat led them to a secluded table and took their orders for lobster cocktails and roast pheasant, following Ian's suggestion. "Just to show that you can cook it better," he had said. With the entrée came a bottle of Batard-Montrachet, 1947, a rich full-bodied white wine. Ian was delighted to find that vintage available as it was one of his favorites. He and Carol clinked glasses in an unspoken toast that said more than words could have expressed.

Ian was talking now in a serious vein, pensively twirling the stem of his wine glass between two fingers. "Did you know that the men in this country don't allow their wives to work?"

"I had heard as much," she replied. "Except for the peasant women. They work as hard as the men—or harder."

"Right. But I was talking about the educated people. You know, sometimes I think they're sensible to keep their women at home. Marriages so often break down if the wife has an independent life of her own. Do you think it chauvinistic of me to believe that?"

"Well, women's lib wouldn't agree with you," she said cautiously.

"But what about you personally, Carol? Would you want to work after you got married?"

"I'd hate to give up my job, I must admit. But it would depend a lot on the man I married." He said nothing, so she went on, knowing it to be true. "If I loved my man enough, I would give up anything for him."

"I believe you would," he said. "But I doubt if there's a man alive who would deserve that kind of sacrifice."

"I might find one," she replied, smiling over the rim of her wine glass at him. "And when I do, I just hope he wants me, too."

After dinner they strolled hand-in-hand through the moonlight along the edge of the river. Trees rustled overhead in a faint breath of air, and the skyscrapers on the far bank glinted from their windows the reflection of a myriad stars.

At the end of the walk he stopped and looked hungrily into her eyes. Her heart throbbed with yearning as her body pressed against his, and his mouth, anxious, exploring, passionate, worked its determined way over her own. In unrestrained response she reached back to him until, on the brink of total blackout, she had to draw breath. Then she clung to him, her head nestled under his chin, her disoriented brain repeating over and over the words she longed to hear, "I love you! I love you!"

But no words were exchanged. They walked back slowly to Ian's car and drove through the nearly deserted streets toward the house to which she hated to return. How much better it would be, she thought, if the Muñoz family had never crossed their path! But they had, and Juanita, if she knew about their evening together, would bring down the full force of her revenge. And if Ricardo knew, he'd tell Juanita.

"Ian," said Carol, lifting her head from where it had been lying on his shoulder while he drove, "I've got a favor to ask of you."

"After that kiss," he said, "I would give you the earth."

"Don't tell Juanita about our going out together when you get back to Iquitos tomorrow. Don't tell Ricardo either, though I don't think you'd be likely to do that."

She sensed his body stiffen. His hands gripped tighter on the steering wheel. "Why not? Not that I'm in the habit of broadcasting the details of my private life, but I don't see why you're suddenly so worried about Ricardo knowing."

"Neither of them must know because one would tell the other. I can't tell you why. You *must* trust me."

"You're sure you're not doing a Carmen?" he said coldly. "Making sure you can keep Ricardo on tap as well?"

"Oh, Ian, I swear I'm not. I thought Manuel had persuaded you of that. He told you it was purely one-sided."

"You could have put him up to it," said Ian stubbornly.

"That's absurd! Ian, you don't think I was play-acting

with that kiss, do you? You mustn't make so much of a simple request."

"Then why mustn't Ricardo know we went out? I don't see . . ."

"Neither Ricardo nor Juanita. It's terribly important, I promise you. Please don't spoil our evening by arguing about it."

"All right," he said resignedly, his tension relaxing. "But I still can't see what difference it makes . . ."

"Thank you," she said replacing her head on his shoulder. "We won't talk about it anymore."

But they didn't talk about anything any more until Ian pulled the car up outside the front door of Manuel's huge, gaunt house. He got out and came round to open Carol's door for her. She stole a glance up at the three rows of windows, but all were dark.

"Thank you for a lovely time," she whispered.

He took her in his arms and gave her a last embrace. "Good night. I'll see you tomorrow. Do you want me to come and pick you up?"

"No, I'll meet you at the airport for the ten o'clock flight."

"Whatever you say." He gave her a last look of incomprehension. Or was it mistrust? At any rate, seconds later he was gone.

Carol crept through the front door and tiptoed up the stairs, carrying her shoes. Silently she shut the door of her room behind her and threw her hands in the air in front of the full-length mirror. Her reflection beamed back at her, the picture of a very happy girl. The small note of dissension in the car was not enough to cast a pall over the evening. Tomorrow it would be forgotten.

She bounced into bed like a child who has been given a long-awaited treasure. Soon the real world blurred into a fabulous, blissful dream . . .

Chapter 8

"Come on, wake up! You haven't time to waste."

Carol's dream became a nightmare and then stark reality as she brushed the sleep from her eyes and saw Juanita standing at the end of her bed, dressed all in black, smart for the city, with a regal turban adding to her height.

"What . . . what are you doing here?" Carol stammered.

"I flew in last night while you were out flagrantly disobeying my orders. I'm here to put an end to your wily schemes once and for all."

"I . . . I . . ." Carol struggled into wakefulness.

"Don't try to deny it. I saw your sickening exhibition with Ian on the doorstep at one o'clock this morning. And Ricardo tells me you were out all night two nights ago—also presumably with him."

Carol flared at Juanita's insinuation. "I was at the . . . Oh, why bother? You wouldn't believe it anyhow." She sat up, pulling the bedclothes up to her neck, glaring at Juanita. "How did you know Ian was in Lima? Ricardo didn't know."

"Well, when I hadn't seen him for over a week, I started making inquiries . . ."

Carol's brain started ticking; she was wide awake now. "So he didn't call on you last Sunday, the day you phoned me at Marilyn's. You were lying to me—again!"

Juanita shrugged her expressive shoulders. "So what? Anyway, that surly Antonio told me he'd taken Ian straight from the camp to the airport, and I knew Ricardo had gone with you and Dr. Todd to Lima. It wasn't hard to guess. Now tell me which hotel Ian's at."

Carol hesitated. "I see no reason why I should."

"It doesn't matter. I'll soon find him. There are only a few big hotels in Lima. Perhaps you'll tell me how long he plans to stay?"

Carol realized that Juanita didn't know as much as she pretended. Manuel must have feigned ignorance. She said haughtily, "He'll tell you himself when you see him." A glance at her bedside clock told her it was already after eight. In an hour Ian would have checked out. Maybe Juanita wouldn't think of the Hotel Pax until it was too late—it was select, but only one of dozens of small hotels in the city.

Juanita saw her look at her clock. "Yes, you'll have to hurry, you obstinate little brat. Because I want you on the ten o'clock flight to Iquitos."

Carol stared. That was the flight she and Ian were going to take anyway. But Juanita was going on, pacing the floor now in her elegant black boots. "Yes, you're lucky. I'm letting you pick up your luggage at Marilyn's before you leave."

"Leave? Leave where?"

"Leave the country? Tonight." Juanita snarled her order.

"Leave the country? You mean you . . . ?"

"That's right. I warned you. I phoned my friend the minister of immigration just now. You'll be arrested if you're still anywhere in Peru tomorrow morning."

"I don't believe you," Carol shot back defiantly. "You're bluffing. You told me you had pull over your Uncle Manuel, and you don't—none at all. He doesn't even like you. You're a big liar!"

Juanita pursed her thick red lips. "Manuel's not as easy to manipulate as he used to be, I agree. But I never thought I'd have to *use* the threat of Ian's license to bring you to heel. I didn't think you'd be cruel enough to him to risk it. It just shows how little you care for him . . ."

"Don't say that! I love him, and I'm going to save him from you if it's the last thing I do. You and your phony threats . . ."

"You'll find out how phony they are when the police come for you tomorrow morning."

Carol had to admit that Juanita sounded confident. And Manuel had told her that the minister of immigration was putty in her hands, or words to that effect. She stalled. "Maybe I can't get out of Iquitos tonight."

"Yes, you can. There's a plane to Manaus in Brazil at four. You better be on it. From there you can go on to New York. You've already got your return ticket. And incidentally, if you don't believe I'm serious, you may as well know that Ian's horrid little Indian girl is back in the jungle already. I arranged it with the school before I came here. She's been expelled."

"Ian won't love you for that."

"He'll never know I had anything to do with it. But he'll thank me when he sees me pull strings to get her reinstated. I'll do that as soon as you're safely out of the country."

"How mean can you get?" Carol hissed. "Trading a kid's future!"

Juanita laughed hollowly, "I can plan, that's all. And you had the nerve to think you could outsmart me! Come on, you scalawag, pack your bag and go. The jails in this country aren't very comfortable, you know."

"What would I go to jail for? I haven't done anything."

"Some trumped-up charge. Anything will do. It'd be a month before you'd even come to trial; justice is slow here. By that time it would be far too late for you to meddle any more with my plans for Ian."

The truth of this statement was undeniable. The newspapers were full of reports of prisoners being held on suspicion. Carol decided she'd better play it safe and go to Iquitos this morning as planned. Then if she found that Juanita's claim about Chicua was true, she would have to assume the other threat was also and go on to Manaus and New York. There probably wasn't much she could do about either Ian or Chicua from there, but she certainly couldn't do anything from a prison cell.

"All right, I'll go." Carol started getting out of bed, and Juanita, with a final contemptuous expletive, left the room.

Carol dressed and packed in ten minutes. Then she started looking for her purse. A brief search convinced her that it was nowhere to be found. With horror she remembered that she had held Ian's lovely, curly head in both her hands when she kissed him good night on the doorstep and that neither hand had been encumbered by her purse. She recalled having it with her after the restaurant in Ian's rented car, so that was where she must have left it, in the car which he would be driving from his hotel to the airport any minute now.

The purse and her lipstick didn't matter, but also in it was Ricardo's valuable ring—*that* she had to return to him before she left, regardless of how she felt about him personally. She would feel terrible if she had lost it.

Nobody saw her leave the house; she made sure of that by slipping out the back way. Out on the street again, she started running. If she'd had any money, she'd have taken a taxi, but her last few dollars had gone on the opera tickets. Fortunately the Hotel Pax wasn't far away, and she arrived breathless in the quiet, dignified lobby well before nine o'clock.

Assuming an innocent, casual air, she walked across to the gilded gates of the elevator, and took it to the fifth floor. She had no trouble identifying Ian's suite—it had an embossed crest on the door—and she only hesitated a second before giving it an urgent rat-a-tat.

Ian was having his breakfast at the same table where Carol had drunk champagne last night. "Hi, Carol," he said briskly but not unpleasantly. "I thought you were going straight to the airport."

"I didn't have enough money for the taxi," she replied, not wanting to appear overanxious about the purse. Knowing Ian, he might chide her for her forgetfulness.

"And didn't want to borrow any more from *him*." Ian always tried to avoid using Ricardo's name these days. "I'm glad to hear that. We'll pick up your bags on the way; there's plenty of time. Sit down and have some coffee."

She poured herself a cup as he went on. "I phoned the hospital this morning. You'll be glad to know Henry had a good night and is doing fine. So we'd better get back to work. How many villagers do you reckon still haven't been immunized against measles?"

Carol thought for a minute. "About two hundred at the most."

"Good. If there've been no new cases by the time we get back, that means the epidemic is beaten, and there's no need to do the rest. So you'll be able to help me collect the last data for my study. Two more days at Pucallpa should do it. This time you've no reason not to come."

It was on the tip of Carol's tongue to tell him the whole story of Juanita's vengeance, particularly now that Ian's license wasn't in danger, but something held her back. His mood this morning was a little cool—after the way he had let his hair down last night, he probably wanted to cover his embarrassment by becoming the efficient physician again, dealing with his nurse. There was still plenty of time to discuss whether she should go to Pucallpa with him or not.

What was more, she could hardly tell him it all without revealing that Juanita was here in Lima, at that moment probably on the phone trying to track him down. That information might precipitate a confrontation with her, something Carol preferred to avoid. Her best tack right now was to get them both on that plane as fast as possible. But first she had to recover the ring and give it back to Ricardo.

"Ian, did you by any chance come across anything in the car after you'd dropped me last night?"

He took a mouthful of coffee before answering. "Oh, you mean your purse. Yes, it's over there." He pointed to a sideboard on the far side of the room; her purse was sitting on its highly polished surface.

"I'm glad you found it. It was stupid of me to forget it."

She sauntered over to the sideboard and picked up the purse. Ian wasn't even watching when she opened it to check the contents. Everything was still in there, including the ring. Casually she came and sat down again, the purse on her lap. "We'd best get going, Ian. If you'll just drop me at Manuel's house for a moment, I'll run in and get my bag." She planned to leave the ring somewhere for Ricardo if he wasn't around, and escape without wasting a second.

"There's time," he said, spreading marmalade on another piece of toast. "I hope you didn't mind my looking inside your purse. It could have belonged to someone who had rented the car before me."

"Oh no, that's all right," she said. "Well, shall we go?"

"I found something in that bag which rather surprised me," he said, making no effort to leave. "A very expensive ring, which looked like an engagement ring to me."

"Oh, that . . ."

"I find it rather odd that you should still be carrying around the ring your ex-fiancé must have given you. When engagements are broken off, the girl usually gives the guy his ring back."

"Well, actually . . ."

"I know it's not really any of my business, but I must say it rather put me off when I found it . . . Carol, you're not thinking of going back to that man in Albany, are you?" His voice had an edge of doubt in it that probably accounted for his cool demeanor.

"Edward? Oh no," she said emphatically. "That's well and truly over."

"Good. It's just that you seem reluctant to burn your bridges as far as men are concerned. So I was wondering whether this Edward might be still waiting on the sidelines in Albany for your return. You can't blame me for thinking that."

"Ian, that's not Edward's ring at all. If you must know, Ricardo gave it to me . . ."

Ian's coffee cup froze halfway to his mouth. With infinite care, he put it down again. "I see." His words cut the tense silence like a knife. "In fact, I see a lot of things now, Carol. I see why you didn't want Ricardo to know we went out together last night . . ."

"It wasn't Ricardo, it was Juanita who mustn't find out, cried Carol. "Perhaps I'd better tell you the whole story. You don't know what I've been going through . . ."

"I can guess," he said bitterly. "Deceit is a tricky game.

It must be awkward to find yourself wearing one man's ring when you're on your way to a date with another, as I imagine you did last night. You'd naturally pop it in your purse. And if Ricardo knew you'd been out with . . ."

"Forget Ricardo, Ian, please! It's Juanita who mustn't know."

"Because Juanita keeps him informed about you and me, that's why. You're right, Carol. She spoils things for you, doesn't she? For example, it was she who told me why you moved into Marilyn's house—so that you could see as much as you wanted of Ricardo without my knowing about it."

"That was a complete lie. Ian, Juanita's a terrible liar. I hate to say so because I know you're fond of her, but now you must know before it's too late. Juanita's been threatening me with all the awful things she'd do if I went on seeing you. Dreadful things! For one, she'd talk her uncle into taking away your medical license . . ."

"That wasn't Juanita—it was her rotten brother. Don Manuel told me so himself. In fact, you were in his library at the time."

"No, that was different; Ricardo had his own reasons for wanting you to leave. You see . . ." Carol started to explain, but it was too confusing. In his present state of mind, he'd never grasp it. "Another thing she said she'd do is have Chicua expelled from her school . . ."

Ian's eyebrows shot up, "Chicua? Expelled? But she's the best pupil in her class. Carol, you're dreaming up ridiculous accusations against Juanita; either that or you're going out of your mind. I can see the two of you not getting along—you're such different types—but this!"

Carol forced herself to be patient. Everything depended on her getting Ian to understand. "Ian, you must listen. She's going to have me arrested if I'm not out of the country by tonight. Now do you believe me?"

Ian's icy calm turned to exasperation. "Now I *know* you're crazy. Crazy for men, the more the merrier. Thank heavens I found out in time. I was beginning to get hooked myself, but not anymore, I can assure you. I'm just relieved I got out of your clutches unscathed. I've no wish to be another notch on your hatchet, Carol. Well, I'm off now. Good-bye."

He started gathering his suitcase, his wallet, and his raincoat together in preparation to leave. "I don't care if I ever see you again."

Carol tugged at his sleeve. "Ian, wait! I'm coming with you. Juanita's here in Lima. You must listen to me! Juanita's in town, do you hear me, looking for you. If she finds me with you, she'll blow her stack."

He shook his head at her sadly. "All the more reason for us not to stay together. With me gone you'll have less to fear from her raging tirade," he added sarcastically, shaking himself free from Carol's grasp.

"Ian, if you leave me here, you'll wreck our last chance . . . I'm going to have to fly to Manaus tonight, and then go on to New York. Juanita will have won . . ."

"Well, you know what they say—may the best man win. I guess it applies to women, too." With that he picked up his new calf-leather suitcase and walked out of the room. Carol stood, rooted to the spot, until she heard the elevator doors clang behind him. Then she threw herself into one of the soft chintz armchairs and stared blankly at the wall for she knew not how long.

She was aroused from her blank reverie by the buzz of the telephone in the room. Automatically she picked it up and said hello.

"So you're there with him, you little hussy," rasped Juanita's voice. "I'm coming right over." The line clicked ominously.

Carol came quickly to her senses. Forty-five minutes till the Iquitos plane left, and she had no money for a taxi. So she had no hope of catching it. But Juanita was on her way to the hotel. She must go at once and hope to get the next flight out to Iquitos.

Clutching her purse she went out through the hotel lobby into the street. Juanita would be coming by the direct route, so Carol cut through the back alleys to Manuel's house. When she got there, she would at least be safe from her tormentor for a few minutes.

In the house she found Manuel was out, but Ricardo

was in the library, reading. Fetching her suitcase from her room, she put it in the entrance hall and went in to see Ricardo. The scene would be difficult, but nothing compared to what she had just been through.

"Ricardo, I'm leaving now. I'm afraid I'm going to have to give you your ring back. Here it is."

He rose from his chair and came over to her. He took the ring, turned it over in his hand once or twice—and then he smiled. Carol hadn't expected that.

"Thank you, Carol," he said, "I . . . er . . . was rather hoping that would be your decision. It makes it easier for me to say what I have to say."

Carol stared at him. He looked decidedly uncomfortable.

"I fear I was a little hasty," he said, clearing his throat. "On mature consideration, I have come to the conclusion, perhaps as you have, that a marriage between us would not be a success."

"Well, Ricardo, you're a nice man. I've always felt *that . . .*"

"And you are a beautiful woman," he cut in. "But it seems that you refuse to be tamed. If I may say so, you fail to understand the prime role of a wife . . ."

"*Your* wife, you mean," said Carol. "And you've found someone else who does understand that role?"

"Yes, I have," he announced ponderously. "The impeccable Francesca has made me the happiest man in the world. I was foolish to overlook her for so long. I hope you will forgive me my mistake."

"Of course, Ricardo. We all make mistakes at times. No hard feelings at all, I promise you. May I wish you every happiness."

"Thank you, my dear." He planted a paternal kiss on her forehead and wished her every happiness herself, a kind thought but one that sent a shudder through her body, coming at the moment when her whole world was collapsing around her.

"Ricardo, would you do something for me before I leave?"

"If I can." He sounded dubious.

"Will you lend me the taxi fare to the airport?"

"Indeed I will." He pulled out some bills and counted out the equivalent of six dollars. "No, five dollars will be enough to take you to the airport," he murmured to himself, putting one of the bills back in his pocket. "You have no need to repay the debt."

"Thank you very much," said Carol, putting the remainder of the cash into her purse. "Say thank you to your uncle for me, will you. Maybe we'll meet again some time."

"I trust we will," he replied, sitting down with a sigh in his chair, and picking up his book, obviously as anxious as she was to bring the encounter to a close.

Carol, almost in a daze from the speed with which things were developing this morning, left the great dark mansion with her suitcase and was soon en route to the airport in a taxi.

She had missed the plane that Ian had been on by half an hour, but there was another flight to Iquitos at noon. Waiting in the terminal, she suffered from a combination of depressing sensations. The threat of imprisonment scared her, and her acceptance of Juanita's demands humiliated her. But she held fast to the hope that Juanita was bluffing, that Chicua was still in school, and that she would be able to catch up with Ian either at the Muñoz villa in Iquitos or at the camp and be able to prove to him that neither Edward nor Ricardo meant anything to her. How she longed to recapture the carefree spirit of their last night of fun!

The plane landed in Iquitos in driving rain, such a change from the dry, desert air of the coast. She had two hours to make up her mind whether to catch the flight to Manaus or not. That depended on whether Chicua was still in school; if she was, then Carol could reasonably ignore Juanita's other threat and stay on in Peru. If not, she couldn't risk it; she would be on that four o'clock flight to Brazil.

She hurried to Marilyn's house, and as good luck would have it, her friend was at home. "Marilyn!" she called, coming in through the door, "I'm back."

Marilyn fussed around getting coffee and cream cakes and then sat Carol down on the sofa, eager to hear all the news. She had heard that Juanita had suddenly flown to Lima yesterday, and rumor had it that she was following Ian.

Carol quickly disposed of Ricardo by telling Marilyn that he had fallen in love with a very suitable Peruvian girl called Francesca, and wedding bells were probably not far off.

"But what about you and Ian?" asked her hostess, agog with excitement.

"There's something I must ask you before I tell you about that. Say, Marilyn, have you heard of a little Yagua girl called Chicua—at least that's her nickname—who is going to the convent school here?"

"Yes, I have, and it's funny that you should ask, because I happened to be talking to the Mother Superior yesterday, and she was all upset because it seems that the board of governors of the school have kicked her out."

"So it *has* happened," said Carol almost to herself. "What reason did they give, do you know?"

"They said her Spanish wasn't good enough, but Mother Superior says that's ridiculous, as the child speaks the Yagua language and is fluent in English as well. They were so proud of her at the school because she was the only Indian, and terribly bright."

"Who are the board of governors?"

"Well, the head of it is a local investment man; one of his big accounts is the Muñoz estate as a matter of fact. Why are you so interested in this little girl?"

"Her father works with Ian at the camp. I've met them both."

Carol's brain moved into high gear at the news about Chicua. So Juanita's threats were not all idle. That meant it was Manaus for her on the next flight or, in all probability, jail. It also meant no chance of seeing Ian again, unless he was still at the Muñoz villa. She asked Marilyn if she could use the phone, and called the villa. Yes, Dr. Morrison had been there that morning, but had left a short while ago for the camp. Putting down the receiver,

Carol flung herself back onto the sofa and gave one of the cushions a vicious punch.

"Carol!" exclaimed Marilyn. "What's the matter? Will you please tell me what's going on?"

"I'm sorry," said Carol apologetically. "I guess things have piled up on me in the last little while. I'll try and control myself."

"Why, what is it? Perhaps I can help."

Carol quickly decided what to say. "All right, Marilyn, here it is in a nutshell. I'm flying to the States in about ninety minutes. Ian has fired me. Actually, my immunization job is finished anyway."

"Fired you? Why on earth would he fire you?"

"My cooking's not good enough for him. Especially pheasant."

"Don't fool with me, Carol." Marilyn sounded a little annoyed. "Did you and Ian have a row in Lima?"

"Yes, sort of. He thinks I keep too many pots on the stove at once."

Marilyn smiled. "I understand what you mean. And *do* you?"

"No, I certainly don't. But Ian doesn't know much about cooking. He smells dishes that aren't there."

"Oh, you poor thing!" Marilyn sounded sympathetic now. "And you're still in love with him, eh?"

Carol nodded and bit her lip. She would have liked to confide the whole story to Marilyn, but she *was* after all a friend of Juanita's, and what good would it do? The whole episode was over, and the sooner she left, the better.

"I'll get over it," she smiled bravely. "It was only a silly infatuation anyway. Well, I must get moving; I've got to pack my things upstairs and go to the bank and draw out my money and get to the airport. And I haven't got long!"

Marilyn followed her to her room, plying her with more questions, but Carol evaded them all. She wouldn't even explain where Chicua came into the picture—anything she said might possibly damage the girl's chances of being reinstated by Juanita. Carol was about to squash her blue backless silk dress into her bag when she realized she would never want to wear it again, whereas the caftan would always bring back memories of a perfect evening.

"Here, take this, Marilyn," she said, pushing the blue silk at her friend. "I never want to see it again. This is the dress I was wearing when . . ."

"When Ian was kissing you and you ran away?"

"That's right," said Carol, busily going on with her packing. "That's the one that started it all."

"You have got it badly, haven't you. It doesn't sound like a silly infatuation to me. Would you forgive him if he came back to you?"

Carol stopped packing and stood quite still for a minute. "Yes, of course I would. You see, it isn't really his fault at all. Juanita has won, that's all. She played her hand better. And had better cards."

"I don't agree she's better for him," said Marilyn, still holding the limp, shapeless wisp of material that had been the dress. "Listen, Carol, why don't you give him another chance? Go up to the camp and talk it all out."

"He's not at the camp. He'll have taken the canoe up to Pucallpa to collect the last bits of information for his study. That's what he told me he was going to do."

"Pucallpa?" Marilyn's voice rose an octave. "He'll never be able to get up there now—not for three months. It's been raining ever since you left for Lima, and that whole country is completely flooded. Those little creeks have become rushing torrents—Pedro was telling me yesterday."

"You don't think he'd try, do you?" Carol felt the blood draining from her cheeks. "You know how keen he is about that study. He might drown."

"I'm sure he wouldn't," Marilyn reassured her. "So why not go up and see him? He'll need some consolation if he's had to abandon his project."

"He doesn't want *me* for consolation," she replied bitterly. "Juanita's the expert at taking a guy's mind off his work."

Carol's temptation to risk imprisonment and rush up to the camp to make sure Ian was all right nearly overcame her. But then she remembered the look in his eyes when he had left her in that hotel room this morning—they had been full of contempt, even loathing—and she couldn't bear to face that look again. No, Ian was lost to her forever. She would have to pick up the pieces and start again. And a jail cell in a strange country was no place to start doing that.

She kissed Marilyn a warm good-bye and carried her suitcase round the corner to the bank. There she drew out the money in her account and took a taxi out to the airport. The loudspeaker was just calling the flight to Manaus as she walked in. Quickly she checked her bag and joined the queue of passengers at the gate.

When she handed in her passport, the immigration officer hesitated and then beckoned her into a back room. A more senior official looked at her photo in the passport and then at Carol herself. Terror nearly overtook her. Was she going to be arrested after all?

But the official merely smiled and stroked his mustache. "I have my orders from the ministry, señorita," he said. "Although I do not understand why such a *chica bonita* should not be permitted to return." He put a large rubber stamp in her passport, filled in some of the blanks in ink, and signed it with a flourish.

He handed the passport back to her, saying, "You may not return to Peru for six months. *Buen viaje,* señorita."

Breathing easily again, Carol passed on through and boarded the plane. Through the window she looked out at the rain pelting down on the tarmac. Beyond the airfield she could just make out the muddy waters of the Amazon. Twenty miles up there, deep in the flooded jungle, she was leaving her heart. And she wasn't allowed to return for six months. Without many recriminations, she hoped that Juanita's manifest charms would be sufficient to make Ian happy. Otherwise her sacrifice would have been made in vain.

Though not really in vain, she thought to herself. Chicua's education was assured now that Carol had left. All Carol had had to give up was the chance to try for Ian herself, the chance to make herself available if he should want her. Although her heart went cold at the thought of leaving Ian to the mercy of Juanita's seductive traits, Carol felt a warm glow about the choice she had made.

In Manaus she checked into the same hotel where she had stayed before. She would have to stay two nights, she discovered, because the New York plane didn't leave until the day after tomorrow. She changed for an early dinner and went down to the dining room, not looking forward to eating alone under the inquisitive eyes of the traveling salesmen who occupied most of the other tables. So she took down with her the book she had been reading on and off throughout her trip and opened it as soon as she sat down.

Out fluttered the black orchid Ian had given her at the camp, the one she had worn to Juanita's party and later pressed inside the book. What vivid memories it brought back, lying there on the white tablecloth, its inky hue still vibrant and mysterious!

The waiter came up to take her order, but started when he saw the flower. "Excuse please, señorita, but where you get black orchid?"

Surprised, Carol looked up, ready to cut him short. But he was an older man, and his expression showed such concern that she said, "A friend gave it to me. He picked it himself. Why do you ask?"

The waiter shook his head and muttered something about it being very bad. Pressed by Carol, he told her in halting speech, as though he was passing on some dreadful tidings, that people in Manaus considered black orchids to be very bad luck. They were used to cast evil spells over enemies by hiding them among the hated one's belongings, and if someone received a black orchid from somone else who wasn't already an enemy, they would soon fall out and become distrustful and cold.

Carol was not usually an easy prey to superstition, but the waiter looked so worried that she asked him what the natives did to destroy the bad vibrations between the donor and the recipient.

"The flower must be burned at sunset," he replied with conviction, "and the ashes must go back into the river, where evil spirit lives."

"You're sure that will dispose of the emnity between the person who gave me this orchid and me?" she asked him.

"It will, unless it is too late," he muttered, and went shuffling away, as if anxious to put distance between himself and the offending blossom.

After dinner she took her book and strolled down to the tree-lined park near the river. There, making certain that she wasn't being observed, she put a match to the dried flower at the moment when the flaming red sun disappeared over the horizon. It flared up momentarily and became a small heap of gray dust. Scooping up the remains of what had been a precious gift, she dumped them over the parapet into the sluggish brown water below her.

The ashes disappeared immediately, and Carol walked slowly back to the hotel in the twilight, hoping that Ian would at least not continue to harbor his present bad opinion of her through the years to come. Even if she never saw him again, it would be nice to think that her love had not been reciprocated by hate.

Next morning she mooned aimlessly around the town. Having nothing to do, she was unable to banish her feeling of despair. Life seemed nothing but a hollow vacuum now, her past little more than a series of regrets, her future of no immediate interest. The cheerful optimism on which she had always prided herself refused to spark; she couldn't even muster any enthusiasm for her return to the States, her family, her friends, or her work as a nurse.

She tried to rest on her bed during the heat of the afternoon, but relaxation wouldn't come; she dressed again and set off once more to pace the streets. She came to the great stone opera house where she had first met Ian, not knowing then who he was. Although she expected the empty auditorium to worsen her depression, she went inside to escape the searing heat of the sidewalk.

Unconsciously she chose the same seat she had been sitting in when Ian had made his surprise appearance on the stage. But this time, even after ten minutes, no entertainers came to fill the bare, wooden expanse in front of her. No lights went on—the opera house remained in semidarkness. But her mind did play one trick on her; she began to hear from the upper reaches of the rafters a ghostly male voice singing arias from Bizet's *Carmen*.

Carol sat there as if in a trance, listening to the familiar songs, letting her thoughts run on unchecked, tracing every detail of the good times she had had with Ian, and recalling with sadness those times which had not been so good.

Gradually the music seemed to come closer; then for a brief period it stopped altogether. Carol waited, her body tense, hoping for it to start again so that she could continue her strange, fantastic daydream. When it did start again, she jumped out of her seat. For the voice was right behind her, bellowing in a rich tenor her favorite of them all, the "Toreador Song."

She whipped round, and there, cutting off the song in midair, arms flung apart to greet her, was Ian himself. For a long moment she stared at him, not daring to move in case the vision should evaporate. But then he spoke and she knew that it was real.

"Was that better than last time?" he grinned. "Or is the rude man again disturbing your peace?"

"Ian!" she cried, flying into the arms that were waiting to enfold her. "Ian! It's you! You're here—I can't believe it." She buried her face in his chest while he smoothed the back of her silky head. "I can't believe you're here. Why are you in Manaus? What does it all mean?"

Gently he eased her back so that he could look into her eyes. "It means that I've come to collect my property—if my property wants to be collected. I've only got Marilyn's word to go on for that."

"Marilyn?" she said, confused. "Marilyn's word for what?"

"Well . . . that little bird told me that I would find a young lady in Manaus who would like to see me again, in spite of the absolutely rotten way I've treated her. Of course, if Marilyn was wrong . . ."

"No! No, she wasn't wrong!" Carol clung to him as though he might run off. "Of course I want to see you again . . . and again and again and again. I love you, Ian. Did Marilyn tell you that?"

"Yes, she did. She had to work hard to persuade me it

was true, but I finally believed her. So I came, because I love you, too."

"Whoopee!" she cried, flinging her arms round his neck and reaching for his mouth with her own.

When they drew apart from the kiss, Carol drank deeply from the tenderness in his gray eyes for the length of time it took to regain her breath and then said, as if talking to a patient, "Now suppose you sit down and tell me all about it."

"Yes, nurse," Obediently he sat down in the nearest seat and pulled her onto his knee. "Would it be all right if we talked like this? I find it more comfortable."

Carol snuggled against him and said, "Well, it's a bit unusual, but this is going to be an important case history, and if you prefer it, I'll allow it just this once. All right, fire away!"

"I don't know if I fell in love with you right here in this old building or a little later, but at any rate, by the time I'd caught up with you in Iquitos, I knew I was sunk."

"You loved me *then*?" Carol stared at him. "You certainly didn't behave like it. You were terribly rough on me at first."

"Overcompensation, I guess," he said with a little sigh. "I didn't really want to hurt you, my darling, but I felt that you must never know how I felt—at least not as long as we were working together."

"And I was for working purposes. You told me. I'm glad I'm not anymore. It was no fun at all."

"Well, anyway, that first night you were at the Muñoz villa, I heard Ricardo making advances toward you on the landing, telling you to call him if you needed anything and so on. So after you'd gone to bed, I went up and told him to lay off you. He argued a bit at first, but then I told him that I'd fallen for you already, and he gave me his oath that he'd leave you alone."

"So that was the trust he broke, was it," she mused. "Funny, Don Manuel said he thought it might be to do with me. I never dreamed . . ."

"Of course Ricardo was pretty mad about it; he had me all paired off with his sister. For reasons of his own."

"Yes, Juanita . . ." said Carol. "She was out to get you all right. I thought she had nearly succeeded. She's terribly attractive."

"I thought so, too," he grinned, "until I met you. After that it was no contest. But I couldn't have you knowing that."

"I see." She paused, and then went on, "Now tell me about what happened in Lima. Why wouldn't you let me explain about that ring?"

"Because I was crazy with jealousy, I suppose. Now Marilyn tells me Ricardo's going to marry some Peruvian girl. That's when I realized I still had a chance with you. I do have, don't I?"

"Try me," she said with a naughty smile.

"Carol darling, will you marry me?" He said it with no hint of facetiousness, sincerely, as if not sure what her answer would be.

Carol could hardly believe her ears. She had expected her spontaneous little challenge to be met by some jocular retort, not a serious proposal of marriage. It made her mind stagger.

She laid her head on his shoulder, trying to bring everything into focus, unable to speak . . .

He seemed to comprehend her confused state of mind. "I'm sorry, darling, I'm rushing you. You must forgive me. But I've had that question buzzing through my head for so long that I couldn't hold it back. Of course you haven't even considered what it would be like to be married to me. I'll give you time to think before I ask you again."

"It . . . was rather . . . sudden," she whispered. "It's not that I don't love you, Ian, you know that. I adore you. But I just wasn't prepared for you to ask me . . . I never thought you would. You've come round to it so quickly. Remember the last time you saw me, you never wanted to see me again."

"I know. I was so blind with jealousy when you told me that you had Ricardo's ring . . . Anyway I was so mad at you that I didn't believe a word you said about Juanita— about her being in Lima, about her threat to you over

Chicua, about you having to leave Peru last night or be arrested—I didn't believe a single word of it."

"How did you find out?" Carol's world was materializing around her again now.

"Well," he was saying, "when I got back to Iquitos, I went to the Muñoz's to change my clothes before heading up to the camp. The butler there told me Juanita had gone to Lima. That started me thinking. And then when I found Chicua at the camp with Jutai, in tears because she'd been kicked out of school, the penny dropped, and I realized you'd been telling the truth all along. Will you forgive me?"

"You aren't to blame. So then I guess you talked to Marilyn, and she spilled the beans about me?"

"That's right, bless her gossipy little heart. I was too late to catch you at the airport—actually I saw your flight take off and thought I'd have to chase you all the way to Albany . . ."

"You'd have done that?" Carol giggled. "How exciting!"

"Of course I would. I wasn't going to let you get away again! In a way it was a good thing my having to wait till this morning. It gave me a chance to arrange something which will surprise you . . ."

"More surprises? What is it this time?"

"You'll see. Waiting for today's plane meant another night at the Muñoz villa. Juanita came back from Lima before I left this morning."

"And she didn't make you change your mind?"

"No way! She confessed to having threatened you when I put it to her straight. It explained why you ignored me at Marilyn's house, and why you wouldn't come to Pucallpa again, something I couldn't understand."

"Didn't she try to work on you this morning before you left?"

"Not really. She didn't love me a bit, you know. And when she saw it was hopeless, she got quite nasty. But there's one funny side to it. She had to make a deal with her sugar daddy, the minister of immigration, to arrest you if you'd stayed in Peru. And the deal was that she would go with him to the Mardi Gras carnival in Rio next month."

"That's not a bad bargain. I'd love to go . . ."

"But not with the minister. She made the deal because she reckoned she'd be married to me by then, which would make it impossible. But now she has to go and spend ten days dancing with a little butterball of a man who's old enough to be her grandfather."

"Serves her right," said Carol, laughing, but then a very serious thought came to her. "What about poor little Chicua? Juanita was going to exert her pull over the school to get Chicua reinstated if I left the country. Now she probably won't, just out of spite to you."

Ian didn't answer, and Carol suddenly felt terribly guilty. Now it was poor Chicua who was going to be sacrificed, not her. Ian eased her off his lap now and led her by the hand out of the opera house into the sunlit street outside. Without a word he guided her one block, and then into a small Brazilian restaurant. Sitting at a table, tucking into some undescribable dish of stew and vegetables, were Chicua and her father, Jutai.

Chicua jumped to her feet as soon as she saw Carol. "Carolina!" she cried, "Ian said you might be here. I'm so happy to see you."

"I'm happy to see you, too," said Carol, bewildered. "And Jutai. But what are you both doing here? If this is Ian's surprise . . ."

Father and daughter grinned knowingly at each other, while Ian provided the explanation. "They're coming to New York with us—I mean they're coming with me—no, I guess it *is* with us, as you're going to New York, aren't you, Carol?"

"By a strange coincidence, that's what my ticket says," she admitted. "Chicua, that is good news. I was worried about you. Are you going to school in the States?"

"Yes, Ian says I'm going to a real nice school where I can learn my lessons in English. It'll be fun, and I can't wait to play in the snow. Maybe I'll become the first Yagua skier!"

Carol laughed. "Skis and a grass skirt would be something to see. You'd be a real Amazon then."

"And Jutai is coming to work in my Tropical Diseases Institute," Ian put in. "His experience will be very valuable, as long as he doesn't start using his witch doctor cures."

"Not all bad," said Jutai, giving Carol a shy look and handing her a bottle of purplish liquid. "I bring you love potion, nurse-lady. Maybe you need in America."

Carol peered into the murky contents of the bottle and crinkled up her nose. "Thank you very much, Jutai, but I don't think I'm going to need it."

A look of understanding passed across Jutai's face, while his daughter gaped open-mouthed. "Me very happy for nurse-lady. And for Señor Morrison."

"Well . . ." said Chicua with a note of sadness, "if Ian won't marry me, I'd rather he married Carolina than anyone else in the whole world."

"That's right, Chicua," Ian grinned, "you work on her. I'm trying as hard as I can. I'm still waiting for an answer to *that* question."

"You're doing well," said Carol, taking his arm as they left the two Indians to their meal. "Where are we going to eat? That is, if you'd planned on us dining together."

"Well, I'm staying in the same hotel as you are, and the food is quite good there . . ."

"I accept your kind invitation, Dr. Morrison," she said, rubbing her cheek against his shoulder as they strolled along.

"Good. By the way, I brought with me a certain blue dress that Marilyn said she thought you might need. It wouldn't fit her, she said. If I get it for you, will you wear it tonight?"

A couple of hours later Carol met Ian in the dimly lit bar of the hotel. In his white suit he looked as superbly handsome as on the night of the Muñozes' party. He rose to greet her when she walked up to him, feeling as though she owned the world, in her barebacked blue silk dress and new high-heeled shoes. His eyes told her how he longed to take her and own her totally himself; the frankness of his gaze set her pulse racing and sent a glow through her whole body.

Throughout the dinner of filet mignon and ice-cold champagne, they talked little, feasting instead on each other's closeness. Afterward, they strolled down to the little park by the river, where only last night Carol had burned the black orchid.

"With nobody to interrupt us," he said softly, "we can carry on where we left off the last time you wore that dress." She sank into his arms, yielding herself completely to the urgent stroking of his hands on her skin as he kissed her with all-consuming desire.

"There's only one sad thing," said Carol wistfully as they leaned over the parapet a few minutes later, taking their last look at the great river that had brought them together. "You never had the chance to finish your study because of the flood waters."

"But it *is* finished," he replied. "All I have to do is write up the report. The results prove my theory conclusively."

"How *can it* be finished?" she asked. "You told me yesterday morning you had to canoe back up to Pucallpa to collect the last data. You even asked me to go with you. Why did you say that if you had all you needed already?"

"Because Pucallpa was the only place I could think of where I could get you alone. I hoped you might be a bad, bad girl again."

"I don't have to go way out into the jungle to be *that*," she smiled. "Not as far as you're concerned anyway. Not now—or ever!"

"I take that as the answer to my question at last," he said with a deep sigh of relief as they walked together slowly back to the hotel.

Dell Bestsellers

- [ ] **TO LOVE AGAIN** by Danielle Steel $2.50 (18631-5)
- [ ] **SECOND GENERATION** by Howard Fast $2.75 (17892-4)
- [ ] **EVERGREEN** by Belva Plain $2.75 (13294-0)
- [ ] **AMERICAN CAESAR** by William Manchester . . . $3.50 (10413-0)
- [ ] **THERE SHOULD HAVE BEEN CASTLES**
  by Herman Raucher $2.75 (18500-9)
- [ ] **THE FAR ARENA** by Richard Ben Sapir $2.75 (12671-1)
- [ ] **THE SAVIOR** by Marvin Werlin and Mark Werlin . $2.75 (17748-0)
- [ ] **SUMMER'S END** by Danielle Steel $2.50 (18418-5)
- [ ] **SHARKY'S MACHINE** by William Diehl $2.50 (18292-1)
- [ ] **DOWNRIVER** by Peter Collier $2.75 (11830-1)
- [ ] **CRY FOR THE STRANGERS** by John Saul $2.50 (11869-7)
- [ ] **BITTER EDEN** by Sharon Salvato $2.75 (10771-7)
- [ ] **WILD TIMES** by Brian Garfield $2.50 (19457-1)
- [ ] **1407 BROADWAY** by Joel Gross $2.50 (12819-6)
- [ ] **A SPARROW FALLS** by Wilbur Smith $2.75 (17707-3)
- [ ] **FOR LOVE AND HONOR** by Antonia Van-Loon . . $2.50 (12574-X)
- [ ] **COLD IS THE SEA** by Edward L. Beach $2.50 (11045-9)
- [ ] **TROCADERO** by Leslie Waller $2.50 (18613-7)
- [ ] **THE BURNING LAND** by Emma Drummond $2.50 (10274-X)
- [ ] **HOUSE OF GOD** by Samuel Shem, M.D. $2.50 (13371-8)
- [ ] **SMALL TOWN** by Sloan Wilson $2.50 (17474-0)

At your local bookstore or use this handy coupon for ordering:

DELL BOOKS
P.O. BOX 1000, PINEBROOK, N.J. 07058

Please send me the books I have checked above. I am enclosing $ _____
(please add 75¢ per copy to cover postage and handling). Send check or money
order—no cash or C.O.D.'s. Please allow up to 8 weeks for shipment.

Mr/Mrs/Miss _____

Address _____

City _____ State/Zip _____

Love—the way you want it!

Candlelight Romances